A MAGIC TOUCH

Memory Guild Book 1

WARD PARKER

Mad Mangrove Media

ISBN: 978-1-7345511-6-7

AUTHOR'S NOTE

The city of San Marcos, the setting of this tale, was inspired by St. Augustine, Florida, a truly unique and magical place. However, I wanted lots of *supernatural* magic! And monsters, too! So I created the alternate world of San Marcos. While some details and historical references may seem familiar, San Marcos is entirely fictional, as are all the characters, names, and places described herein.

CHAPTER 1
LIMPING HOME

"As the Carpet King, I promise our prices are so low they'll floor you! That's the Knobble Family Flooring guarantee."

I shut the car radio off. I'd been hearing Knobble commercials since I was a child. Over the generations, the family's taste in advertising hadn't improved one bit, nor had their taste in flooring. Hearing the ad meant I was getting close to my hometown, San Marcos, Florida. I was returning to start all over again, definitely older and hopefully wiser. I was half a century old (rounding down), toughened with the battle scars of life, but still naïve enough to believe I deserved to be happy.

My name is Darla and I talk too fast in run-on sentences, and I really, really promise I'll try to avoid that with you. My first husband didn't have the mental capacity to understand much of what I said at normal speed, let alone when I was in a manic state. Husband number two could keep up, but had a hard time getting a word in edgewise.

That might have been one of the reasons he up and left, though why would you leave a wife just because she talked too fast and too much? He didn't have any other complaints that he mentioned.

When I'm depressed, I barely talk at all.

The exit to San Marcos was a mile ahead, so I moved into the right lane. I normally avoided driving on I-95, but I was traveling from Key West, a nearly 500-mile trip up the peninsula of Florida, too long a journey to do on local roads. I had driven overnight to avoid traffic. Doing so felt almost as if I were sneaking away from my failed experiment of trying to hang onto the bed-and-breakfast inn I ran with Cory before he bailed on me. I had learned it's too hard to run a mom-and-pop shop when it's just mom.

During the long drive, I endured long sequences of memories. As I came closer to my hometown, they bubbled up as strongly as the mythical Fountain of Youth that was once believed to exist around here.

After I exited the highway, I headed east, first through the countryside with farms and trailer parks. Then came the gated subdivisions, varying in age and price. As I approached the city, I passed the car dealerships, shopping centers, and big-box stores, lots of billboards, telephone poles, and palm trees. So far, my surroundings could be anywhere in Florida.

But as I continued eastward, the examples of human habitation grew older. Some sections were seedy and run down. Others were quaint and charming. All were built long before I was born.

Returning to San Marcos was a process of going back in time, literally and metaphorically. I wasn't just returning to my hometown and my past. I was also entering a city that never fully existed in the present. San Marcos was laden heavily with history. It had witnessed centuries of European settlement and millennia of Native-American before that. My personal dramas that took place here were drops in the ocean of my city's memories.

The city of San Marcos was like an ancient family member who passed the time as a faded retiree. It had secrets it shared with only a favored few. It had scars and resentments and long stretches of forgetfulness. It also had its proud moments of glory, as most cities do, yet these moments were more ancient and enchanting than those of any other city on this young continent.

Nowadays, its moments of glory survived only in memory and museums. But San Marcos continued to soldier on through the centuries, trendy new boutiques and restaurants coming and going, while the city's true strength came from all the human stories that were its sustenance.

San Marcos was technically a city, but a small one. Its population was barely more than ten thousand. I skirted the outskirts of Spanish Colonial Old Town, which huddled tightly with its memories, its ancient structures hidden by the Victorian-era buildings that surrounded it. Those late-nineteenth-century homes lined the street I now followed. My mother's house, where she and my twenty-four-year-old daughter lived, was up ahead in what only in San Marcos could be called a newer neighborhood. I turned off the main road onto her street.

I wasn't returning to my hometown to make my life easier. I had to deal with my disaster case of a daughter. And if that wasn't daunting enough, what did I do? I saddled myself with enormous debt, buying a 285-year-old inn, that needed extensive work, to open it as a bed-and-breakfast.

Was I completely nuts?

Yes. That's a fact, Jack. Being occasionally telepathic didn't help, either. I never knew if the voices in my head were real or not, whether they were my inner demons talking or the guy in line behind me at the supermarket. You see, the paranormal runs in the family. Not just me, but Mom and her mom. I didn't yet know if my daughter Sophie inherited the gene.

3

Mom's house was now in view down the street. It was our family's home, where I grew up, but now it's just Mom's. The large yellow Victorian didn't have a visual focal point. It was an explosion of rounded turrets, gabled roofs, bay windows, ginger-bread trim, and a wrap-around porch.

When I grew up, my father was a real estate broker. My mother was a homemaker. And a witch. In the prehistoric era when I was born, it was common for wives to stay home with the kids. She also stayed home with magic spells and the occasional summoned spirit. When my sister and I grew bored with our games, there was always a poltergeist to entertain us.

Dad had been normal. His passions were sports and selling homes, and he didn't have a drop of the paranormal in him. He tolerated Mom being a witch because she mostly practiced it when he was at work. To him, it was a silly hobby, and she pretended to agree. She concealed enough of it to convince him the witchcraft was nothing more than Tarot cards and incense burning.

My younger sister was also normal. She was an excellent student, stayed out of trouble, and eventually went to law school. She currently lived in California with her husband, two kids, and two dogs. Her holiday cards consisted solely of professional photos of her perfect family in their perfect home. She didn't even write anything on the cards.

Then there was me. The weirdo. The weirdness I inherited from Mom, along with the paranormal genes. I don't think I inherited anything from Dad except for my bipolar disorder, but that's a story for another day.

Dad died from a heart attack when I was thirty and still married to Mr. Degenerate, husband number one. With no kids at home to support, Mom took the insurance money and most of their savings and blew it all on antiques. Our rambling home had always been teetering on the brink of becoming a hoarder's paradise, because of Mom's love of buying "bargains" at thrift and antique stores. She'd said she planned to resell them, but never did.

Now, with cash to burn and no husband to stop her, she surrendered to her acquisitiveness and filled the home with more stuff. Much more. She didn't have a singular style or theme; she bought everything that fancied her from any era. With the house filled to bursting with furniture, art, knick-knacks, and jewelry, she hung a sign out front and called it an antiques store.

On its rickety wooden front porch I stood and rang the doorbell which was literally a series of silver bells connected by strings.

My daughter Sophie answered, her beautiful milky skin threatened by tattoos creeping up from under her blouse, now reaching her lower neck. The neck ink was new. She had straight, black hair like mine. It fell upon her shoulders when she turned her head, covering the offending tattoos.

She smiled to see me, which was a good sign, and we hugged. A few random thoughts of hers popped into my head, concerned about how I was holding up a year after Cory left, whom she loved as much as her own father.

"You're up early," I said.

"It's ten o'clock, Mom."

"Early for you."

"Not when I'm working. I got a job at that new seafood place on Front Street. I'm working lunch today, so I need to leave soon. How long are you staying here with Grammers and me?"

I noted the way she said, "Grammers and me," as if they co-owned the house. Mom had generously offered to let Sophie stay there until she could afford her own place in San Marcos. So far, she'd been staying there for nearly a year.

"I'm only staying here tonight. Then I'll stay with my friend

Danielle in Old Town until I close on the inn and my stuff arrives from Key West."

"Should be fun. Come in, and I'll help you with your bags. Then I have to do my face and go to work."

Sophie and I had been close when she was a girl, but had drifted apart since then. Because of my telepathy, she wanted to be as far away from me as possible when she was a teenager. What teen wouldn't want to avoid a mother who could read her thoughts?

She fell in with a bad crowd in high school, and I stupidly allowed her to go to the community college in San Marcos instead of sending her off to another state where she'd have to make new friends. So she'd had problems at times with drugs. And boys. And holding down a job. Maybe it was for the best that I was back in town.

"Is that you, Darla?" Mom's voice called from the back of the house.

"Hi, Mom," I shouted in reply.

The bottom floor of my childhood home had a lovely parlor in front, overlooking the porch. Next was a formal dining room which flowed to a large living room, and finally a huge old-fashioned kitchen. A butler's pantry led from the kitchen to the dining room. The ceilings were tall with crown molding. Wainscoting covered the lower portions of the walls. The home was brimming with Victorian-era charm.

But now it overflowed with junk.

Our original furniture was probably still in there somewhere, hidden by all the new pieces, display cases, bookcases, and random junk like a milking tub and a wagon wheel. It was the same in each room I passed through. There didn't seem to be any system of organization. If you were looking for an Art Deco lamp, you would have to search every single room of the house. I was afraid of what I'd find upstairs.

The kitchen seemed like the only sanctuary from the encroaching tide of junk. It was cluttered, of course, but there was actually room to sit at the table or on a barstool beside the giant island.

I expected to find Mom here, but the room was empty. I poured myself a cup of coffee from the coffeemaker that had survived decades.

"Have a seat," Mom said, striding into the room and hugging me. "Let me get you a scone."

Mom had our family's distinctive jet-black hair. Hers had long ago gone to gray, but she dyed it an unnatural black like the original. While Sophie and I had straight hair, Mom's was frizzy and surrounded her head like the corona of the sun. She had a splotch of white paint on her cheek.

"What were you painting?" I asked.

"A rattan dining set I found put out by the curb a few blocks away. How someone could throw away something in great condition like this set is beyond me. It needs painting, though."

Mom's instinct for junk acquisition hadn't faded.

She brought a plate to me with three of her homemade scones. She was famous for them. In fact, she often mixed certain herbs and powders into the batter, performed a spell while they baked, and claimed they had love-inducing qualities. All you had to do was feed them to your love object and by the time he or she had digested their meal, they'd be madly in love with you. Word on the street was that they truly worked. I reserved judgement until I tried them out myself on an unsuspecting man. That might be my only hope at this point.

After she set the plate down, Mom hugged me again and kissed the top of my head.

"Welcome back to San Marcos. How was your drive?"

"Exhausting. I did it in under eight hours."

"You know, you can stay here until you move into your inn.

You don't have to stay with Danielle. I mean, she lives in an apartment above her store," Mom said, as if Danielle's living arrangements were a scandal.

"That's okay, Mom. Thanks for offering. But it will be fun to hang out with Danielle, now that we're both single women again."

"I know you feel like this house is too crowded. Maybe I do have too much stuff."

"It's not just crowded with stuff. It's crowded with Chesswick women."

"You can stay in my room if you don't want to sleep in the magic room."

"It's not that. I told you I want to hang out with Danielle. Get together with Jen. Drink too much wine. Not have to worry about being a bad example to my daughter who's in recovery."

"Ah, I see." Mom nodded furtively.

It sounded awful trying to blame Sophie for my not wanting to stay here. That wasn't the entire reason. I simply didn't want this to feel like the forced cohabitation you endure when families gather for the holidays. I didn't return to San Marcos to eat turkey. I came here to begin a new life as an independent woman.

"Mom, you hate it when I remind you, but I'm fifty-two. Danielle is forty-nine. We won't go crazy and invite boys over. If things are too wild, I know your sewing room is waiting for me here."

"Magic room."

"It used to be your sewing room. I'd rather sleep in a sewing room than a magic room."

"They're just hobbies, dear."

"One of those hobbies made my prom dress. The other one turned the mailman into a sex addict."

"Daughters blame their mothers for everything."

8

CHAPTER 2
BAD MEMORIES

Danielle Lieberman had been a grounding force in my life since middle school. I looked forward to staying with her. Rather than spend money on a hotel while simultaneously offending my mother and daughter, I had accepted Danielle's generous invitation to stay with her in her apartment above her rare coin shop in Old Town, essentially downtown San Marcos. After my obligatory night sleeping at Mom's house, I couldn't wait to stay with Danielle.

The shop was a block from Royal Avenue and all the touristy restaurants and T-shirt shops. Prince Street was paved in cobblestones and barely wide enough for a car to pass through. Some buildings dated from the sixteen and seventeen hundreds, with second stories that jutted out over the street below. It was quiet and shady along here, and you could imagine yourself in those earlier eras. Only the modern signage of the high-end jewelry and antique stores spoke of contemporary times.

Lieberman Rare Coins and Collectibles was in the middle of the block. It looked like a small jewelry shop, but the coins, medallions, and snuffboxes in the window were behind double-thick, bullet-proof glass. You had to ring a doorbell for Danielle to buzz you in.

It was 10:35 a.m. The store opened at 10:00. I pressed the doorbell.

No response. I tried again with a similar result. Peering through the thick glass of the door, I didn't see Danielle. The lights were on inside.

Without thinking, I pushed on the door. The latch clicked, and it opened.

That was odd. Had Danielle turned the security system off? If so, why?

I pushed the door wider and stuck in my head.

"Danielle? Hello?"

An uneasiness grew in my stomach. Something was wrong here. I went into the store and looked around. Nothing seemed amiss. All the antique coins, jewelry, and personal items made of gold and silver, glass and pewter, were in their display cases. Nothing looked disturbed.

Until I saw the spilled coins in the rear of the shop, in the doorway to the back room. I followed them like breadcrumbs into Danielle's storeroom and office.

My friend lay on her back in a puddle of blood next to an open safe. Her long, blonde hair was splayed out in the dried blood like the rays of the sun in a crimson sky.

I didn't scream. I guess I had been girding myself for the worst. And that was what I found.

Heart pounding, I crouched, avoiding the blood puddle, and touched Danielle's neck, feeling for a pulse. There was none. Her skin was cold. Her body looked stiff, as if in rigor mortis.

My stomach convulsed once, twice. I staggered to the small bathroom in her office and knelt before the toilet. I didn't throw up, but the convulsions from my stomach spread throughout my body as if I were having a seizure.

The spasms wracking my body were my sobbing.

I lay on the bathroom floor and cried for the loss of my friend. It wasn't the sadness of losing someone dear to disease or accident. I was old enough to begin hearing news, still blessedly rare, of classmates from high school dying.

No, what bothered me was the loss of Danielle to murder, to some punk who killed her while stealing rare coins. Who swatted her away like an insect that was in his way of getting easy goods to sell at a pawnshop.

Danielle was kind and gentle, smart and funny. She wasn't disposable.

My grief turned to anger, and that was a good thing, because the anger didn't hurt as much. It made me want justice and vengeance. It gave me strength and resolve.

And it stopped me from cowering in the bathroom. I steeled myself, and returned to the back room to survey the crime scene.

My guess was that she had been killed by a blow to the back of her head, because that appeared to be the source of the blood. I couldn't see a wound, since the back of her head lay against the floor, but her skull was misshapen where it touched the tiles.

I guessed she had been killed the night before and had lain here overnight.

Several felt-lined trays were scattered about inside the open safe and on the floor. Coins of gold, silver, and other metals sprinkled every surface. It appeared that the burglar had taken little, since he had left so much behind.

I removed my phone from my back pocket to call 911, but my hands were shaking too much, and I dropped the phone. It clattered on the tile.

Damn. I was a mess. When I bent to retrieve the phone, something odd caught my eye. Danielle's mouth was tightly closed, but a tiny bit of a gold tooth protruded onto her lower lip.

The problem was Danielle didn't have a gold tooth.

I bent closer to see what it was. I knew I shouldn't have, but I touched her lower lip, pushing it down slightly.

There was a coin in her mouth with the crude markings of an ancient one.

Had Danielle hidden the coin in her mouth so the intruder wouldn't find it? This must be a truly special coin.

The curiosity was too much. And the anger, too. A burglar had murdered my friend, and she had died hiding this coin in her mouth. I had to see it, crime scene evidence be damned.

I touched her lower lip again. Her jaw barely moved, but as I disturbed her lip, the coin slid out.

Okay, I admit it didn't just happen. I helped the coin slide out onto her chin.

Having grown up in San Marcos, I knew a lot about Spanish antiquities. They built this city in the fifteen hundreds, and archeologists were still finding their relics to this day.

I was familiar with the silver *reales* and gold doubloons often found in shipwrecks from the colonial era. Danielle had several for sale. They could be quite pricey, depending on their age and condition. But none was rare enough to protect by hiding it your mouth when a murderer was searching your stuff.

This coin was different, though. Some silver showed along the edge, indicating the gold had been applied onto a silver coin. That was odd. And the markings on the gold surface didn't look European; they appeared to be Mayan or Aztec. Instead of the profile of King Philip, there was a skull.

Sometimes, modern jewelry makers add stuff to antique coins, but this looked original. And there were no hooks or anything to suggest that someone had turned this coin into jewelry. It looked authentically from its era.

Had the intruder been searching for this very coin? Or was it just so special that Danielle didn't want it to fall into his hands?

There was something compelling about the coin, even for a girl like me who wasn't into jewelry and precious metal. There was an energy—a force—in it. My innate paranormal senses prickled.

I wanted to take it. But that would break all the rules.

Feeling dizzy, I reached out and grabbed Danielle's desk to steady myself. My hand brushed against a metal object. It was a bronze figure of a cherub, about ten inches tall.

Was that blood on the base of it—and hair? Too late to stop myself from leaving fingerprints, I touched the statuette.

And a freight train of psychic force walloped me. It felt like I'd been knocked into the next zip code, but my hand still touched the bronze. I couldn't see anything. And then, I wasn't me anymore. I was—

—holding the chubby bronze angel in my right hand, while the shopkeeper was writhing on the ground in pain after my boot to her stomach. Good thing she wasn't a screamer. I've made her show me every single coin in this store and not one of them was the one I sought.

I know it had been here. She had made the mistake of listing it in an auction manifest, obviously not realizing its true value. Not knowing the powerful forces that sent me on a years-long mission to find it.

She said she'd sold it just the other day. I don't believe her. But I've searched every inch of this store without success. And she wouldn't have known to hide it. She had no idea I was coming.

"One last time," I say. "Give me the name of the buyer."

"I told you I don't know," she says, panting heavily. "It was a cash sale."

In truth, there really wasn't any reason for her to lie to me about that.

And there wasn't any reason to let her live.

She sits up on the floor. And I slam the bronze cherub into the back of her head, and again. That was more than enough to do the job. And then—

—I forced myself to let go of the bronze cherub, and I was myself again, leaning against the desk, my dear friend dead on the floor.

What the heck just happened to me?

Like I said before, I had a bit of the paranormal in me, so I knew whatever I just went through was probably paranormal-related, not a schizophrenic hallucination.

But still, I was losing it. First, finding Danielle, and then this.

Touching the bronze figurine had triggered it. As I thought about what I had just experienced, I realized the killer had held that same figurine before he used it to kill Danielle. I was reliving his thoughts and sensations.

It was as if his memory was attached to the cherub. Somehow, I had relived his memory.

As my heart slowed to a less-panicked rate, I pulled myself together and called 9-1-1. I told them I had found my friend dead and that the store appeared to have been robbed. I mentioned nothing about the coin and the statuette.

While I waited for the police to arrive, I stared at the angel, partly to avoid staring at Danielle. The cops would easily determine that the angel was the murder weapon. They would find my fingerprints, too. Which wasn't good. I needed an alibi for last night. And they might not find the murderer's prints if he was wearing gloves. In fact, my sensations from his memory told me that was the case.

The angel wasn't of much use to the cops. But it might be useful to me. If I could learn some clues to his identity.

I reached my hand toward it, then hesitated. I didn't want to go through that experience again. But the cops would be here any minute. I had to do this now. So I touched it.

And relived the same event again. But as the killer's thoughts dominated my mind, the tiny part of me that was still me tried to glean what had been in his subconscious mind and other layers of data in other lobes of his brain. I sensed it was there, but I struggled to get beyond the angry, brutal thoughts that dominated him as he decided to kill my friend. And as he swung the first blow, I was able to let go of the angel and end the horrible vision before the blow landed.

The only additional thing I learned was that he was visiting from out of town. I needed more information, and I realized I would have to relive the murder of my friend to the bitter end until this monster's physical contact with the bronze was completely finished.

So I tried one more time. And it was gut-wrenching and nauseating at the same time. I stayed with it through each smack of the bronze against the back of Danielle's head, with the horrible sound it made, the disgusting feel of the hot blood spattering.

Until finally, finally, he put the angel on the desk. Thoughts of how to get out of there unseen and how to clean up were already running through his mind.

And thoughts of the route he would take to his hotel, with a quick flash of the image of the front of the building. His memories then switched off, and I could pull myself out of the trance.

I had scored one small win: I recognized where he was staying. A cheap chain motel in an undesirable neighborhood a few miles from downtown, where the tourists with little money or no reservations spilled over.

Flashing lights outside filled the window. I glanced one last time at the angel whose surface was now covered with my fingerprints. I knew that trying to wipe them off would probably get me in even more trouble. I'd already broken enough rules.

I gave one last look at my dear friend who hadn't deserved to die like this. It was all because of that coin resting on her bottom lip. A coin that someone wanted badly enough to kill her when she didn't give it up.

What was so special about that coin? Was it simply the dollar value based on its rarity? Or some other significance?

I wondered if the coin would reveal to me any of its secrets.

So, yeah, I sure did break all the rules. I grabbed the coin and put it in my purse.

CHAPTER 3
THE CHANGE

T he cops told me to get out of their way and sit in one of the easy chairs in the front room, or "gallery" as Danielle called it. So I called Mom and told her what had happened and that I would need to continue to stay at her house. After the mammoth struggle to end the call, I just sat there and stared at the glass display cases. On the walls were antique lithographs from the nineteenth century of scenes of San Marcos tourist sites.

I had given a bare-bones account to the first cop of how I had stumbled upon the murder scene. Next, I was supposed to speak with a detective. In the meantime, I watched a couple of paramedics arrive and go into the back room before leaving, unneeded. Then, crime scene techs arrived and went back there. Soon after, an official-looking older woman, whom I guessed was a medical examiner, joined them.

The detective, who had been in the back room since right after the first cops arrived, finally emerged. He stood in front of my chair looking at me.

"They tell me you touched the murder weapon," he said.

Before I gave my rehearsed speech, I studied him. He was middle-aged like me, but was well into his fifties and I had only just arrived there. I had to admit he was handsome.

They say men's looks are less ravaged by time than ours, but it's not always true. Some guys go downhill not long after being allowed to vote. I would say my first husband was in that category, but I'll save that for another time.

Other guys look more distinguished with age. Or ruggedly weathered in an appealing way. This detective would be in that category. And he was only slightly a victim to the condition most middle-aged guys succumb to: the big belly. Some men have a bit of a paunch on their muscular torso, like Detective What's-His-Name standing in front of me. Some guys are skinny but look like they've swallowed a basketball. The ones with no gut at all I don't trust, unless they're clearly an athlete. Which would be the category of my second husband, the one who disappeared when he figured he could do better than me.

Then, of course, there was the issue of hair, or lack thereof. Detective What's-His-Name was a victor in that war, retaining all his dark, curly locks half turned to gray.

Yeah, overall, he wasn't bad looking. Which was the last thing I should think of while my friend lay dead in the next room.

"I'm Detective Samson. You told the officer your name is Darla Chesswick?" he asked, taking a notebook from the back pocket of his pants. On TV, detectives always wear suits, but this guy sported a fly-fishing shirt. Florida being Florida.

I nodded.

"You told the officer that you handled the angel statue?" He had a slight country accent.

"Well, handled is too strong a word, I touched it, and then sort of tilted it backwards to see what was on the bottom. When I saw what was on it, I didn't touch the angel anymore."

"You realize that if your prints are the only ones on the statue, and it's determined to be the object that caused the victim's death, you'll be a suspect, don't you?"

I knew this was coming.

"There are people who know I was going to stay with Danielle. Why would I kill my host?"

Detective Samson shrugged and jotted a note on his pad.

"And," I continued, "I stayed at my mother's house last night. She can vouch that I didn't leave the house when Danielle was killed."

"The time of death hasn't yet been determined," he said.

"Come on. I'm no expert, but it's obvious that body is not fresh."

I cringed when I realized I'd just said that about my friend.

"We'll let the medical examiner decide that herself."

He then peppered me with questions, a lot of them covering stuff I'd already told the first cop. I had to explain why I left Key West to move here. What time I departed the Conch Republic, why I drove overnight, what time I arrived at my mother's house, what time I arrived here this morning, why I opened the shop's door when no one answered the bell, and what I noticed when I looked for Danielle.

To make a long story short, I left Key West because I could no longer make a go of it with our small inn after my husband bailed on me. Key West was too expensive, anyway. I figured I could be more successful running a bed-and-breakfast in San Marcos. Buying the house online with which I would pursue this venture was kind of weird, but I was already familiar with the house from growing up here.

Why I drove overnight? So I could get through South Florida without the ridiculous traffic. And why I only stayed at Mom's house one night before coming to stay with Danielle? I gave a much-abbreviated version of the truth. And we don't have to rehash what I saw when I came to the shop, right?

"Your mother is Sadie Chesswick?" Samson asked. By now, he wasn't attractive to me anymore.

"Yes. Why?" I asked, though I knew the answer.

"She has quite the reputation."

"Of what?" I would not let him get out of this easily.

"She's eccentric. Not that there's anything wrong with that."

He was referring to rumors that Mom was a witch. She sure as heck was. She came from a long heritage of witches. But the regular humans of San Marcos didn't believe in witches. Officially, that is. And the city's Magic Guild made sure that remained the case. But the fact was, Mom helped friends and neighbors from time to time with spells and potions, amulets and charms. Usually, her magic worked. Sometimes, it didn't. In the "official" way of thinking, the folks who believed in her magic were superstitious souls who thought it would help them win the lottery. Their superstition was fine, as long as it didn't harm anyone.

Like I said earlier, I'm a bit of a telepath. People's thoughts sometimes pop into my head unbidden. And right now, the detective was wondering if I was a kook like my mom. I was probably bipolar and certainly a drama queen, and those were things I didn't want to admit to him. But a kook? I was proud to be one.

I decided to confirm to him I was.

"Would you like some help finding the guy who did this?" I asked.

He raised his eyes in amusement like I was a precocious child.

"We didn't know that a guy did this," he said, "and how in the world would you help me?"

"You said my mom is eccentric. Well, this apple didn't fall far from the tree. I'm a bit eccentric, too. And a bit psychic. Let's just say I'm fairly certain it was a guy."

"Did you see or hear anything you haven't told me about?"

"I had a vision."

He smiled. Yep, he thought I was a nut.

"Thanks for your offer, but we can handle this on our own."

"I really want this case to be solved. Danielle was my friend."

"I understand. I promise you we'll spare no effort to find the culprit."

"I've heard of police departments getting help from psychics before."

"Maybe. But not ours."

"Write this down on your pad," I said. "The man who did this stayed at the Sleepy Inn on Atlantic Street. I don't know his name, or what he looked like, or if he's checked out of the motel."

A memory surfaced in my brain.

"And he wears steel-toed work boots made by Dickies."

"Okay," he said, stretching it out into a three-syllable, mocking tone. But he did write something down on his pad.

"Can I go now?" I asked.

He laughed. "Oh, you give me that gift wrapped in a bow and you're done? Nope. I need you a little longer."

He proceeded to ask me even more questions, most of which covered information I had already told him. But then, he got into personal matters, such as my marriages and if I had any financial debts. It sounded like he still thought I might be a suspect.

Finally, he put his pad back in his pocket.

"*Now*, can I leave?"

"First, one of the techs will take your fingerprints. *Then*, you can leave. Give me your phone number. I'll probably ask you to come to headquarters to talk with me a little more."

Great, I thought. More of my time wasted when I have a business I need to get up and running.

Samson went into the back room, and soon a woman half my age came out. She replaced her latex gloves with a new pair and then read my fingertips and palm with some sort of hand-held optical scanner.

Once she finished, I left, finally. I walked two blocks to where I had parked and got into my car with relief that the ordeal of dealing with the police was over.

The next thing I had to endure was my grief.

"I'M SORRY YOUR RETURN SAN MARCOS HAD TO BE SO terrifying," Mom said.

"It still hasn't sunken in yet. Only the sadness I feel for Danielle."

Mom gave a tight-lipped smile of sympathy. She still looked good for seventy-five. Her chin was dimpled, her nose was pert like mine, and her wrinkles were fewer than one would expect. The reason was magic, no surprise there. I had vowed I'd never learn magic for self-indulgent reasons like my appearance. Now that I've crossed the half-century mark, I'm not so sure anymore.

"I'm trying to keep focused on the closing and beginning work on my new house, you know, but I'm afraid to find out how much it will need. Although, a little work never hurt anyone, wouldn't you agree?"

I was trying to stay chipper. Let my manic side run rampant.

But then, the memories washed over me—the memories of the murderer I had experienced when I held the bronze angel.

"What's wrong, darling?" Mom asked.

"I don't know how to explain it."

But I tried to anyway, with all the details of the buzz I felt when I touched the statuette and how my personal identity went away as I became this other person, this killer. I told her how vivid the visions were, how horrifying it had been.

"Oh, you had an episode of psychometry," Mom said. "It's a paranormal ability to read the psychic residue that people leave on objects they touch. Supposedly, the more intense their emotions are at the time, the more powerful your vision is."

"I've had my little bit of telepathic ability my entire life. But never this. How could I suddenly be able to do this?"

"Menopause."

"Are you serious?"

"Absolutely. Hormones going haywire often trigger new abilities in women who already have the paranormal in them. When I went through menopause, it definitely strengthened my magic." She pointed to the lack of crow's feet by her eyes and smiled.

"But I'm not going through menopause yet," I said.

She scoffed. "That's what we all say when it begins."

"Okay, maybe a hot flash now and then. But that's all."

Mom nodded sagely.

"Will psychometry cause problems in my life?" I asked.

"Only if you let it. You have to learn to sense when an object has powerful memories before you touch it, so you're prepared and don't allow yourself to become too immersed. I've heard that can be dangerous and trap you inside the memories."

"That's kind of what happened with me."

"You'll need to be careful. It could be dicey here," she spread her arms, "with hundreds of antiques touched by countless hands."

"Not hundreds. Thousands upon thousands of antiques are crammed into this house."

"Not crammed. Artfully displayed."

"Whatever."

"You're the one who bought a three-hundred-year-old inn," Mom said. "Maybe, upon reflection, that wasn't the best idea."

"I didn't know about psychometry when I bought it."

"I know. Just be careful. And think of your new ability as a gift. You can do a lot of good with it."

"Like what?"

"Solve crimes, for one."

I had already tried to do that by tipping off Detective Samson on the motel the killer used.

"You see glimpses of history the way it really happened and correct errors in our collective memories," Mom continued. "You can be a guardian of truth and memory."

"You're getting a little too abstract for me."

"I think it's time you looked into the Memory Guild."

"I've never heard of it."

"The supernatural society of San Marcos is organized into guilds. The guilds protect their members, but also regulate them. I'm a member of the Magic Guild. We make sure witches and wizards avoid scrutiny from law enforcement and the press. That magic is done for good, not ill. Prices are regulated and scammers are punished. Black magic and demon summoning is forbidden, and any offenders are driven from the city."

"You never told me you were a member," I said.

"Secrecy is one of the many rules. The Clan of the Eternal Night is the vampire guild. And there are guilds for shifters, immortals, seers, and other people and creatures with supernatural abilities."

"Those are all very specific. What sort of people belong to the Memory Guild?"

"People like you who have psychometric abilities. Mediums who speak with spirits. Reincarnation therapists. Astral time travelers. And some good, old-fashioned scholars without an iota of paranormal abilities."

"Sounds like a motley crew."

"You should join them," Mom said. "It will give you a sense of purpose."

"Purpose? My purpose is to open an inn and try to make it profitable so I can continue to hemorrhage money into my daughter's hands, hoping *she'll* find a purpose."

Mom looked me in the eye. She was all business.

"You've been through a lot in recent years. Sophie is all grown up, even if she can't get her act together. You've reached middle age. Now more than ever you need a purpose so you can get the most out of your life. Now's the time to find happiness. What you said just now didn't sound like a recipe for happiness."

She was right. My outlook had become unnecessarily grim. Grim is my middle name. But that's what reaching midlife without a retirement fund will do to you. All I had to look forward to was working my little butt off and trying to save money. There had to be more to life, and maybe it was time to be open to finding what that was.

"So, Mother, how does one go about joining the Memory Guild?"

"When you're ready, they will come find you."

CHAPTER 4
INN AND OUT

It was only my second day in San Marcos, and here I was being interrogated by the police again. I was about to do a last-minute inspection of the house I was closing on, when Detective Samson called and asked—no, it was stronger than asking—that I come to the police station immediately.

I reluctantly drove there and parked behind the building. I had to wait for fifteen minutes in the lobby. So much for "immediately."

Samson came out and gestured for me to follow him, without so much as a hello. We entered a large, open room with desks arranged in rows. He sat at one of them, and I took the chair across from it.

"What hotel did you say you're staying in?" Samson asked.

"I didn't. I told you I had been invited to stay with Danielle, but then she was, you know. Now, I'm staying with my mother in uptown."

"Have you ever stayed at the Sleepy Inn?"

"Never."

"Why did you tell me you believed the suspect was staying there?"

"I thought I had explained that to you. I had a psychic vision. Well, it's more accurate to say I read his memory."

"I don't understand." Samson looked angry.

"It's called psychometry. When I touched the angel statuette, I read the memories that the murderer left there when he had touched it. It's like I went into a trance and experienced the thoughts he had at the time."

"Sounds like nonsense to me."

"After the murder, he was thinking about his route to the motel and pictured it in his head. I recognized his image of it. I thought this might be useful information for you, but I guess I was wrong."

"No, you were right."

"I was?"

"We obtained the guest registry. An individual with an alias known to us checked in the day of the murder and never checked out. Housekeeping found his room vacant in the morning."

"Oh, so you don't disagree with me that Danielle was killed last night?" I asked, with a little too much of a tone.

Samson glowered at me. "Forensics confirmed it. And, as I was saying, we searched the room and found a bloody footprint fragment. The blood matches the victim's. We don't know why he didn't check out of the hotel before the murder."

Because he hadn't planned on killing Danielle, I thought.

"Did you look to see if this alias is registered in another hotel in town?" I asked.

Samson looked at me like I was crazy. "No. Because he left town."

"Are you absolutely sure?"

After all, the man hadn't found what he was looking for. I had the coin. Of course, I couldn't tell Samson that.

"You should check," I said. "I got the sense when reading his memory that he was seeking something at Danielle's shop but didn't find it."

"What was it?"

"Probably a coin. I don't know," I lied. I felt terrible lying to the police, but I'd already gotten myself too deep into this. I took the coin from Danielle's mouth, which was illegal, and I couldn't admit it now without getting in trouble. More important, I planned to try to read the coin as soon as I had time and privacy.

"I hope you're not withholding information from me," Samson said with a stern glare. In his job, he surely had a sixth sense for spotting liars.

"I promise if I learn anything, I'll tell you at once." And that was the truth.

"I'm not too proud to accept a tip. We'll check out the hotels in and around town. If he's still in town, you'll want to look over your shoulder, just in case."

It was a sobering thought. I didn't know how the murderer would know about me, but if he ever did, I would be in danger.

"I will," I said.

"I'll be asking you back here to talk again. I have a feeling you could be of more help."

That was his polite way of saying he thought I was holding something back. But now that I didn't appear to be a suspect anymore, I wouldn't mind meeting Detective Samson again. He was pleasing to the eye, as they say.

After I left the station, I called my realtor, Jen, and asked her to meet me at the house that was soon to be mine. I knew I was imposing. The closing was tomorrow, and it was too late to make changes to the deal. There was no reason for me to inspect the house now except that I was dying to see it. Buying a house sight unseen tends to do that to you. Fortunately, Jen was an old friend, and her office was nearby, so she promised to be there in ten minutes.

The house, long known as the Hidalgo Inn, was in the historic district of San Marcos, but on its southern edge, in a quiet neighborhood away from the frenzy of the touristy areas. It had been built in the early seventeen hundreds while the city was still under Spanish rule.

It was three stories, with thick walls of limestone made from coquina rock quarried from the nearby beaches. Someone had painted it white years ago, and the paint had worn off from the elements, revealing the brownish gray of the stone. The front wall of the house directly abutted the narrow, cobblestone street. The house was on a corner lot, so the side wall ran along the other street. A tall privacy wall enclosed a large courtyard behind the home. A small swimming pool was supposed to be back there. I wondered where the guests would park, since spaces were very rare in this neighborhood, and many of the streets were too narrow for on-street parking.

"Darla!" said a voice behind me. "It's so good to see you!"

I turned and gave my beaming friend a hug and cheek kiss. Jenny was shorter than me (which was pretty short) and heavyset with short, auburn hair. She seemed to have aged a lot since I last saw her six years ago. I wondered why.

One of the odd things about reaching midlife is when you realize you look like it. When I looked in the mirror, I didn't think I showed my age too much. Maybe it was vanity, mixed with familiarity. It's hard to notice yourself age when you see your face every day. But when I compare myself to photos of me from years ago, it's not too bad. Being petite with good skin and in reasonable shape has helped me, I think.

Seeing Jen, though, was unsettling. She was my age, but

looked like her mother did when we were much younger. It made me realize, yes, I'm getting old. I'm menopausal. I'd better get what I want out of life before it's too late.

"You're looking great," I said, not truly lying, because Jen looked happy despite whatever had rapid-aged her. "How are Frank and the kids?"

"They're wonderful." That was all she said. Maybe the cause of her rapid aging lay with a family issue.

Jen unlocked the lockbox hanging from the doorknob and removed the house key, then unlocked the front door.

"I'm afraid we have to make this brief. I have a showing in an hour. Besides, you'll have all the time in the world to explore after tomorrow."

"I know, of course. I appreciate you indulging me like this. I just had so much anxiety over the condition of the house."

The heavy wooden door opened with a creak, revealing how thick the stone walls were, nearly two feet. This provided a cooling effect for the structure, but the primary reason the house was built like a fortress was that it was meant to serve as a fortress of sorts. San Marcos, a garrison town, had been under constant threats since it was founded in the mid-fifteen hundreds. The French, the English, and pirates constantly attacked the city. The royal government decreed that homes on what was then the edges of town had to be built to double as defense bastions.

I wish my heart was built that way.

Jen stepped aside and allowed me to enter. My first impression: a musty, mildewy smell. My second: boy, is it dark with the shutters over the windows. I reached for a light switch, but the electricity was off. It had been off in the vacant house for years.

My third impression: This place is haunted. Big time.

Yeah, I forgot to mention the paranormal lurking in my innards seems to be a magnet for ghosts. Not that I drew them here. But I was sure I'd draw them out from their eternal slumber.

"I think it's haunted," I said.

"That might be a lovely selling point. People who prefer old inns often have a fascination with ghosts."

"I hope you're right." I wasn't sure she was. It all depended on what kind of ghosts we had here.

Jen had already looked at the place when I did my long-distance negotiations, so I knew there wasn't any major damage. But I still wanted an idea of how much work and cash it would take to get the place up and running. I borrowed Jen's flashlight and took a quick tour of the three floors. There were eleven bedrooms and an additional two in a cottage next door that I was planning on living in myself. One suite occupied a corner of the ground floor where the kitchen, dining and living rooms were. The two upper floors each had five bedrooms. The ones facing the courtyard had balconies.

The good news was the house was fundamentally sound. I already knew that. The bad news was that it needed a lot of cleaning and cosmetic work. It was too dark to inspect the furniture that came with the place. And I couldn't check the plumbing because the water was off. It looked dangerously old, though. Some bathrooms had fixtures and tile that appeared out of the Victorian and Edwardian eras, while others had an Art Deco feel.

In fact, the home had a hodgepodge of architectural and interior design styles that spoke of centuries of renovations by various owners. This was most obvious in the bedrooms, where the difference in styles was deliberate. Some were Spanish Colonial, one harkened to the Civil War era, and several were Victorian-themed. A couple were fairly modern and trendy, though I doubted the kind of guest who preferred that style would choose to stay in a bed-and-breakfast inn.

I wandered back downstairs, aware that Jen was waiting for me to finish. I paused in what once was a parlor or drawing room near the foyer. Here was the reception desk and a small sitting area. What grabbed my eye was an enormous fireplace. The heavy stone mantel looked Medieval and must have been imported from Europe. It even had four little gargoyles supporting the mantel.

I stopped. Did the gargoyle on the far-left move?

No. Impossible. The shadows were playing tricks on me.

"Are you the new owner?" an English-accented voice asked.

I jumped. "Who's there?"

Was this one of the resident ghosts?

"'Tis I. Archibald. I am a gargoyle," a voice said from the fireplace. "Well, technically, I am called a grotesque, because I don't spout water like a gargoyle. But I find the name 'grotesque' rather demeaning. Wouldn't you? I believe myself to be quite handsome, actually. Most people use the term gargoyle for my kind of architectural feature, as well as the water-spouting kind, so I'll just go with the gargoyle identity, thank you. I was originally sculpted in Leeds, but how I ended up in this city is a long story suited for another time."

Sure enough, the grotesque—I mean, gargoyle—on the far left was turning his head, around the size of a cantaloupe, to look at me.

"A gargoyle? But how—"

"Please spare me the incredulity. I spotted the supernatural in you the moment you walked into this house. In fact, word is already spreading that a new psychometrist is in town."

"But I only just discovered I have the ability," I said, wondering why I was talking to a stone face that looked like a demon with its tongue sticking out.

"'Of all the gin joints in all the towns in all the world, she walks into mine,'" the gargoyle said in a decent Humphrey

Bogart imitation. "Actually, this is splendid luck on my part to be one of the first to meet you. Please say you're the new owner of this house."

"I will be as of tomorrow."

"Excellent! And you must join the Memory Guild."

"You're the second person who has said that. Well, second entity. Not to be rude, but I need to ask, how are you able to speak and why do you know about the Memory Guild?"

"To answer your first question, I am a supernatural creature. Not all gargoyles are, of course. Most are nothing more than stone sculptures. I can talk, but only the humans I speak to can hear me. Regarding your second question, I am a member of the Memory Guild. I am a stone-speaker. I communicate with the statues of the city, the stones that built the city, the masonry, the gravestones. If it's rock, it will talk. To me, that is."

"Insane," was all I managed to say.

He ignored this. "You can use your psychometry to touch a brick and read the memories of a human who touched the same brick. Whereas I can read the *brick's* memories."

"How can a brick have memories?"

"Well, 'memories' isn't the right word. Although there are some statues in this city who are supernatural and have more memories to share with you than you'd want to hear. But a normal, inanimate brick retains some of the energies of what has gone on around it. Especially if it has been here for centuries. I can explain it better another time. But do remember this: there is more to history than what humans say and do. And, yes, there's a lot more to this world than humans."

"Okay," I said.

"Now, will you consider joining the Guild?"

"I promise I'll think about it."

"Who are you talking to?" Jen asked, entering the room.

"Don't worry," Archibald said. "She can't hear me. Only you can."

"I was leaving an audio note to myself on my phone," I lied.

"Are you about wrapped up here? I need to get to my showing."

"Yes. It was just a quick walk-through, but I feel better now," I said. "I didn't find any major problems. Except the fact that it's haunted."

And has a talking gargoyle.

CHAPTER 5
THE MAGIC ROOM

D id I mention my mother was a bit of a hoarder? And now
she owned an antique shop, which was permission to let
her hoarding instincts go feral. Those who actually lived in the
house paid the price.

The junk—and let's face it, she didn't sell high-end antiques
—spread through the house like a fungal infection. Aside from
the kitchen, the entire ground floor was taken up by the
merchandise, including the detached garage, a storage shed, and
a gazebo in the backyard. On the second floor, the bedrooms,
including the master suite, were also filled with antiques and
browsing customers. The third floor was where the family took
refuge. Mom had a decent-sized bedroom. Sophie used a tiny
guest room. And they relegated me to what had once been a
sewing room in a turret before it became Mom's magic room.

Yep, the only place for me was a daybed in a room custom-
made to produce nightmares. There was a nineteenth-century
apothecary chest made up of tiny drawers of herbs, powders,
crystals, and parts of insects and lizards. A bookcase, awkwardly
placed against the rounded wall of the turret room, held

grimoires and spell books. The small closet was filled with boxes of plastic containers holding more eerie items. The handwritten labels were faded from age, so I couldn't tell what was within, except for the mummified birds and toads. Some of this stuff probably came from Grandma, who was also a witch.

There was one window, tall and curved, that was the only charming feature of the room. Of course, dark, musty curtains covered it.

This was the only place Mom could put me. And this is where I would have to live until my new inn became habitable. In this room, barely large enough for me and my suitcase, I decided it was time to examine the coin that possibly was the reason Danielle had been murdered.

I opened my purse and removed my wallet. The coin lay on the bottom, next to a pack of chewing gum. The silver *real*, with a gold overlay, had been in the mouth of my friend when she was bludgeoned to death. She had been that desperate to keep it from the thief.

Why? What was so special about this coin?

It was slightly smaller than a quarter, about the size of the hundreds of Spanish *reales* I'd seen in shops and personal collections growing up in San Marcos. It was in good condition, but there was nothing supernatural about it. An aura didn't glow around it, no field of magical energy radiated from it. I could easily imagine it staying forever at the bottom of my purse among random pennies and lipstick tubes.

In fact, I had no confidence that my newly discovered gift of psychometry would work on this coin. I still wasn't sure I believed in the gift at all. I'd always had a knack for examining an object in a thrift store or antique shop and imagining who its previous owners were and the lives they lived. I assumed that flowed from my imagination, nothing paranormal about it.

Maybe my incident with the bronze angel was just my imagination, amplified by the trauma of having discovered Danielle's body. Maybe I didn't have psychometric abilities at all.

But when I remembered the intensity of what I had experienced, I knew that wasn't true. It must have been something paranormal.

I stared at the coin down there in the pit of handbag hell. I didn't want to retrieve it and hold it in my hand.

I was frightened of what might happen.

So I closed my purse and put it on top of my suitcase. I would take a nap instead. Laying down atop the lumpy daybed, I closed my eyes against the late afternoon sunlight that made it past the revolting curtains. I tried to doze off.

But I couldn't. I kept thinking about Danielle. How should I reach out to her family? They had been notified by the police and would take care of the arrangements, but did they know about me?

As I tried to doze, I worried about getting in trouble for removing an item from the crime scene. I wondered what caused my ghoulish act to remove the coin from the mouth of a corpse.

Most of all, I stewed over the injustice of sweet, innocent Danielle being taken from the world.

I really wanted to right this wrong—to help catch the murderer and whoever had sent him on his mission. I wanted to avenge my friend's death. And the only way I could contribute was if my alleged "gift" did indeed work, allowing me to find clues from the coin.

It couldn't hurt to just hold the darn thing in my hand for a few moments, could it?

I got up and grabbed my purse, stuck my hand in and found the coin by touch. I pulled it out and nothing odd happened. The coin seemed unnaturally heavy, but not unusual beyond that.

I sat on the daybed with the coin resting in my right palm. I closed my fingers around it. Okay, now what?

I was hot. The AC wasn't good up here. I began sweating. For some reason, the smell of the ocean was strong. The sun—

—burns the top of my bare head as I stand here with my fellow soldiers. I touch my Beloved in my pocket. It had originally come from the Spanish pigs, from one of their ships we seized. But to me, it has only brought good luck. I pray it does today. I pray it keeps me alive and the Spanish exchange us in a prisoner swap.

Our men move forward toward the shore of the inlet where the next group is rowed across to the other side. Spanish soldiers wait for them there.

When the boat reaches the opposite beach, they march the ten prisoners at the point of sword and pike up the sand dunes and disappear on the other side.

What are they doing to them? We were told they will feed us, but none of us believes them. Yet, we do not mention what the alternatives could be.

I will have to board the boat soon. Sergeant Alvarez seizes my shoulder—

(Flash of light)

—and I fall upon the tiles, pain flaring in my left knee as it strikes the floor. As I gasp, the coin nearly falls from my bra, but I slap my hand against my chest just in time.

I have shown him every box and tray of coins in the shop, hoping that he'll give up. He's rummaging through the safe now. There is more than a million dollars of rare coins inside, but he's not interested in them at all. I sit on the floor watching him sift through the stacks of metal trays, expecting him to palm some and stick them in his pockets. That's what thieves do. Even someone completely ignorant of numismatics would recognize a gold U.S. Eagle coin to be valuable. But he is obsessively single-minded.

All he wants is the Real de Tenochtitlan.

How I regret cataloging it. I knew it is special, so I was proud of it and made it public. But how was I to know how truly remarkable it is? It wasn't until Margaret found the engraved box that had once held the coin.

He's yelling at me again. Why won't he just give up and leave my store? I've cooperated completely.

Oh, God! He's yanking me to my feet by my hair. He's shouting that if I don't give him the coin, he'll torture me. His spittle is landing on my face. He smells like a pig.

For the first time, I get a good look at his face. It's gaunt and unshaven. His nose is slightly crooked, like it had been broken before. Green haunted eyes. His hair is long and greasy, tied in a ponytail. His navy polo shirt bears the logo of a country club he surely doesn't belong to. He's missing two teeth on the upper right side. He's skinny, but taller than me and much, much stronger.

I tell him he can take whatever coins he wants. He shakes his head and screams that he only wants the one coin, and he knows I have it.

He turns away, head swiveling wildly, searching for God knows what. I use the opportunity to remove the coin from my bra and place it in my mouth in case he searches me again more thoroughly. Or does something much worse to me.

He paces around the storeroom as I press myself into the corner, as if it could make me disappear.

He says he's going to be in so much trouble if he doesn't find the coin. He's speaking more to himself than to me.

He roars in anger and slams his fist upon my desk.

His hand wraps around the bronze cherub from the Netherlands. He picks it up, weighing it with his other hand.

He's back in my face, screaming again, spittle raining on my cheeks. He's totally losing it. I cover my face and turn from him.

And a massive blow hits my head. The pain spikes, my vision grays. Another blow. My God, my God, my—

—I was on the floor in the fetal position next to the daybed, head in both hands, crying. The intense pain I had experienced was gone, but the trauma wasn't.

I opened my eyes. Yes, I was in the former sewing room, now magic room. Sun still seeped through the gap in the heavy drapes. The rug atop the hardwood floor smelled musty.

I was not in Danielle's store. Nor was I a prisoner of the Spanish on that beach long ago. I was safe here in Mom's house, where I'd grown up.

But I was haunted by what I had witnessed. By what I had experienced, seemingly firsthand.

My right hand ached, and I realized it still gripped the coin tightly. I forced my fingers open and looked at the coin. It left an imprint of a skull in my palm from being held so tightly.

And it put a mark upon my soul.

WELL. THAT WAS FUN, WASN'T IT? NOT EVERYONE GETS THE chance to experience their friend's murder. And that incident on the beach? Based on the men's clothing and the armor on the Spaniards, that scene took place nearly 500 years ago after San Marcos was founded. The coin pre-dated that time.

I was amazed that I could read 500-year-old memories. If that was the case, how many other individuals have owned this coin and imprinted it with their own thoughts?

I dropped the coin back in my purse. It had my thoughts on it now as well. My secrets and emotions. I hoped I wasn't thinking any naughty thoughts while I was holding it. Because my naughty thoughts would curl the hair of an unsuspecting psychometrist.

I stood up and paced around the tiny room in the turret of our 1883 home. I was surrounded by history everywhere—in this town and this house and in my purse. I was drenched in history.

So many Americans lived in brand-new suburbs that popped up on what used to be farmland. They went shopping in brand-new strip malls in brand-new chain stores, drove brand-new cars and worked in brand-new office buildings.

Their experiences seemed so limited to me in a way. But I imagined it must feel so liberating to not have this heavy cloak of time I had draped over my shoulders at every turn.

My emotions were still in turmoil from my experience with the coin, but I came to a resolution. I was going to ride Detective Samson's butt until I heard the killer was caught. And I would ride it further to make sure he investigated who hired the killer. Maybe I would have to look into it myself as well, though I had no detective skills.

Whoever hired the thief knew there was something special about this coin—not just its age and provenance. The world had plenty of Spanish coins still in existence, so there had to be more to this particular one. I really, really wanted to know what it was.

And I came to an additional resolution. I was going to join the Memory Guild. I didn't understand what it was for, or exactly what it did, but I needed some like-minded folks to guide me in handling this powerful new gift of psychometry. Although, I didn't think "gift" was the right word. It was dangerously close to being a curse.

And I wanted these like-minded folks to help me discover the story behind this coin. That is, if I could call a gargoyle like-minded.

I shook my head at the craziness of it all.

CHAPTER 6
BUYER'S REMORSE

After my closing, I put my new house keys in my pocket and joined Jen for a celebratory lunch. We picked a Southern-revival spot popular with locals. It was downtown, but out of the touristy area, tucked away in the shadow of the old cathedral. We sipped sweet tea and shared a plate of fried green tomatoes while Jen caught me up on some of the town gossip I'd missed while living in the Keys.

"How is Sophie doing?" Jen asked. "I hear she's working at The Wharf."

"She is, and she's doing well, thank you. I have confidence that she'll stay clean and sober this time."

Sophie's addiction problems saddened me, so I was relieved when the entrees arrived, and I could change the subject. I got the meatloaf sandwich and Jen had the shrimp and grits. It was great food, and we didn't care how many calories we racked up.

Halfway through our feeding frenzy, Jen blurted out:

"Danielle's store is on the market already."

"Already? Doesn't it have to go through probate? Well, I

guess it doesn't if she left it to her family in her will, even so, doesn't it take time for all that to sort out?"

"It turns out she wasn't the owner. A company owns the store. I don't know who they are."

I was shocked. Danielle had always been so proud of her business. I knew for a fact that she bought it herself, as well as all the inventory, because I was still living in San Marcos at the time.

"Maybe she had money problems and had to sell it to an investor," I said.

"I thought you'd want to know. Sometimes, our friends' lives aren't exactly what we think they are."

She gave me a penetrating stare. Was she hinting that I was keeping something back? Well, there wasn't any secret love interest in my life. And I was not going to blurt out about my newly discovered power of psychometry, that was for sure.

"Oh no," Jen said.

"What?"

"Look at the hostess station."

There, peering into the restaurant to see if there was anyone he knew, was my first ex-husband, Buddy. Also known as the cretin who wasted my best years. You may know him as "Florida Man," the iconic imbecile who gets in trouble for doing something stupid while drunk and naked which sometimes involves an alligator or a stolen police car. Buddy wore a Hawaiian shirt, shorts, a goatee, and a blow-dried comb-over. He hadn't changed one bit since I last saw him years ago, except his spare tire and the bags under his eyes had grown larger.

I had no ill will toward him anymore. Together, we had raised a wonderful daughter. And at my age, I was more forgiving toward weak humans than I'd been when I divorced him. But I still reserved the right to be judgmental.

He had a beautiful brunette with him.

"Who is that woman?" I asked.

"Esmerelda Methany."

"She's pretty and well-dressed. Why is she going to lunch with Buddy?"

"They're an item," Jen said. "Sorry for you to have to find out this way."

"She looks like she has money."

"She does."

"Then what in tarnation is she doing with Buddy?"

"You're not the first to ask that question."

"I'm serious," I said. "He's costing her money every minute she spends with him. Not just her dishing out cash to that loser, but she's watching the value of her reputation sink."

"I don't have any sort of answer that would please you," Jen said.

"Yeah. So she's not with him for his money. And not for his wit and acumen. Certainly not for his handyman skills. And speaking of his skills, they're also seriously lacking in the bedroom department. Unless he learned some new ones somehow. But you can't teach an old dog new tricks."

Jen wisely remained silent.

"That moron nearly bankrupted me," I said. "I fell in love with him in the ninth grade. And it only went downhill from there. Why did it take me so long to divorce him? Even after Sophie was old enough to handle it?"

Then he saw me. He made a beeline to our table, his voluptuous friend in the expensive sundress in tow.

How was I going to handle this without crude insults or fried green tomatoes flying into his face?

"Darla! What brings you back to San Marcos?" he asked, smirking.

"I fell off a boat, and the Gulf Stream carried me up here."

"I'd like to introduce my fiancée, Esmerelda," he gestured to his friend.

"Darla, nice to meet you," she said with a 150-watt smile. "I've heard so much about you."

"It's what you haven't heard that you need to find out," I said with a 40-watt smile. "How did you two meet?"

"Esmerelda used to be married to the head of Public Works. Who used to be my boss when I worked there."

And I'm sure you had nothing to do with them getting a divorce, I thought.

"This is my friend and realtor, Jen," I said. "I believe you and Buddy already know each other from high school."

"I didn't realize you actually attended classes, Buddy," Jen said.

"You're helping Darla buy a new house?" Buddy asked.

"Your ex-wife is now the new owner of the Hidalgo Inn."

"How exciting!" Esmerelda said with a fake squeal of joy. "I can't wait to see it when you're open."

"It might be a while," I said. "There's lots of work to do, but the sooner I have a cash flow, the better."

Esmerelda looked at me with knowing eyes. But not in the way your scandalous mind is headed.

"I've met your mother," she said. "She's quite a character."

"She is. So is her daughter. As Buddy has surely told you."

"No, no. Buddy has always only said wonderful things about you."

"That's so nice of you to say, Esmerelda. If only it were true."

She smiled uncomfortably. She was lucky that the hostess stopped by and led them to their table, fortunately out of sight.

"After she divorced the Public Works chief, she started dating all these rich guys," Jen said. "She's moved into a luxury townhome near the beach."

"Buddy was no help in buying that."

"She has an event-planning company, but I don't think it's successful. And I haven't heard of any rich relatives dying. So I'll leave it there."

"Yes, do."

After some mindless small talk, and two pieces of key lime pie, we asked for the check. And I walked the four blocks to my new home and, hopefully, future source of income.

THE FIRST THING ON MY TO-DO LIST WAS TO CREATE A TO-DO list. I didn't even know where to start. After I unlocked the heavy Spanish-style oak door, the most obvious task went on my list: set up an account with the electric company. I also needed to open all the shutters, but the ones on the ground floor were secured with metal rods and were locked. Jen said she believed the keys to them were in the house somewhere. The shutters weren't approved hurricane window coverings; they were contemporaneous wooden shutters, painted green, that matched the building's Spanish Colonial style.

A quick search of the kitchen drawers didn't yield any shutter keys. The kitchen wasn't large, but had a quaint potbelly stove as well as modern appliances. It was probably added to the building in the nineteen hundreds. Prior to that, the kitchen would have been in an outbuilding in the courtyard. It looked like the kitchen had been renovated not too long ago, so that was a huge load off my mind.

The upstairs shutters were opened and closed from the inside and were not locked. I went from room to room, pushing them open, and folding them back against the exterior walls, securing each one with a hook that attached to an eyebolt in the wall.

It was as if the sunlight woke the house up from its three-year slumber of being unoccupied. As the light poured into each bedroom, I felt happiness flood into my heart.

I also felt a low hum of energy. It was the psychic residue of the hundreds, perhaps thousands, of people who had lived or stayed here. Mostly, it was positive feelings. But in any structure that held many people over the years, there would be sorrow, anger, and other negative emotions. Fortunately, they were in the minority in my new old home.

The impressions I received were low-level and general. I was certain that if I carefully handled specific objects, I would get more powerful and precise memories of those who had handled them before.

Even the simple act of opening the windows and the shutters gave me brief glimpses of the guests who had opened the windows and of the former owner who had shut them for the last time when he abandoned the house.

I stood in a room on the second floor with a tiny fireplace and, in my opinion, a rather gaudy hot tub that had been added in more recent years. Based on an old brochure for the home's most recent incarnation as an inn, this must be the honeymoon suite.

The vibes I was getting here were, shall I say, on the carnal side. I realized I was blushing with embarrassment in an empty room. Maybe my sex-deprived imagination was amplifying the vibes. I blushed even more.

In every room, I felt the same low hum of past human energy. In many rooms, there was a unique vibe that spoke of powerful emotions having been felt there.

The doors of all the rooms were open, saving me from having to touch doorknobs. Except one on the third floor facing the side street. For some reason, this door was closed.

I hesitated. Then grabbed the knob, turning it—

—and entering the dark room. A single candle is lit atop the bureau,

showing her standing in front of the open window, keeping her back to me. The clip-clopping of a horse and the rattling of a carriage upon the cobblestones below are loud.

She keeps her back toward me, refusing to acknowledge me. Refusing to answer for what she has done. The old anger surges through me. Anger and pain and jealousy.

I want to lash out. Release this anger. And punish her. The urge is so strong, and I can't suppress it as I enter the room and—

—I snapped out of it after I yanked my hand from the door-knob. I was back in the current sunny day.

But, oh boy, some heavy crap had gone down in this room. I didn't want to deal with it now, but I felt obligated to learn more of the story of what happened here. Stories, actually.

In fact, the entire inn was filled with untold numbers of stories. Every home held stories and memories, of course. But older homes hold so many more. And I now had the ability to read some of them. It was exciting, but also scary.

But that would have to wait for another day.

Before I left the room, something odd struck me. The shut-ters were already opened. Since this room faced the street, I would have noticed from the outside that one of the windows was not shuttered. But I hadn't.

So when had these been opened? And by whom?

I BELIEVED THERE WOULD BE AN ATTIC. I WASN'T SURE ABOUT Spanish Colonial homes built in the seventeen hundreds, but English Colonial homes usually did. The problem was, I couldn't find it. There were no stairs leading to an attic, and no trap door on the ceiling above the staircase. I looked for hatches in the ceilings of the five bedrooms on this floor, including in the closets and bathrooms, but didn't see one. Either the attic didn't exist, or had been sealed up. If it had been sealed, the reason would be a story of its own.

I made my way downstairs. The stairs, by the way, were in fairly good shape. Less so between the second and third floors where they were narrower and a bit ricketier, though. Each flight had hardwood treads and was covered with a dark red-carpet runner, anchored by stair rods along the bottom of each riser.

I had been avoiding the front parlor, because I wasn't in the mood for a conversation with a gargoyle. Sometimes, like when you have a lot of practical concerns on your mind, you're just not in the mood to deal with the supernatural. I'm sure you would agree.

But when I entered the room and looked at the fireplace, the gargoyle wasn't there. Three of the ornamental stone creatures supporting the mantel were present, as they should be. They were carved from stone after all. But the fourth, the one on the far left that had spoken to me, was missing, leaving a square patch on the stone that was brighter, having not been exposed to dust and ashes for hundreds of years.

The little bugger had simply detached himself and gone off somewhere. I didn't know where gargoyles spent their free time, so I didn't bother speculating. At least, I had the place to myself for the time being. As long as the ghosts, whose presence I sensed here, didn't wake up.

It bothered me that it was still dark on the ground floor. I had to find the keys to the shutters. The antique writing desk that served as the reception desk was the most logical prospect in here. There were three shallow drawers under the desk surface. The one on the right was divided into twelve compartments which held the eleven room keys. No electronic card keys or apps for your phone in this place. We were decidedly old-school here. Each key was hooked to a small disk with the room number.

The middle drawer held registration forms and the like. I assumed the previous owners had a computerized system as well, but you never know. The left drawer had three key rings with a bunch of assorted keys. Some were labeled. Many, unfortunately, weren't. I breathed a sigh of relief when I saw a pair of duplicate keys labeled "shutters."

Outside, I went from window to window opening the shutters, much wider and taller than the ones upstairs. The locking mechanism of each was at the bottom and operated a rod that ran the height of the left-hand shutter which overlapped the righthand one. This rod slid into the stone wall at the top, and a bolt at the bottom entered the windowsill. The mechanisms were pretty sticky from the salt in the air from the bay and years of disuse, but I eventually got them all open.

Then I studied the other keys. I wanted to get into the cottage where I would be living. I still hadn't seen it yet, since I'd been so obsessed with the income-generating parts of the property. There were also two outbuildings that needed inspection.

I noticed an antique key labeled "wine cellar." This piqued my interest. Cellars were rare in Florida because of our high water table and propensity for flooding if you're near the coast. I wanted to see how deep this cellar went and whether it was usable.

And I'm not going to lie to you, I secretly hoped there were bottles of rare wine still down there.

Now, the question was, where the heck was the door to the cellar? I prowled the ground floor of the building, looking in the obvious places, enjoying the rooms illuminated by sunlight. I didn't see a door in the kitchen or near the dining room. No sign of it in the other rooms either. A walk around the courtyard and the pool area proved there weren't any doors or stairs into the ground. I didn't think it would be beneath the cottage or outbuildings, because they were more recently built. So I went back inside.

I checked in the less-obvious places, like the laundry room, the closet beneath the staircase and other storage areas. I looked carefully for seams in the flooring or recessed draw rings.

Then, a light went off in my little brain that the newer appliances might not be where the original ones were. I peered behind the large industrial-size refrigerator. Nothing was there. Then behind a smaller, standard-size fridge.

Eureka! There appeared to be a low, narrow door in the wall that had been painted over with white lacquer paint.

By this point, I was obsessed, so there was no stopping me. I rolled the fridge away from the wall and examined the door. The large, old-fashioned keyhole was covered by the recent paint. I tried the key and it fit, the bolt sliding with a satisfying click. A lump of paint indicated a shallow handle was beneath the keyhole. I took a small screwdriver that I carry around in my purse (which is not as weird as it sounds since I'm an innkeeper and always need to fix things). I scraped away enough paint to give me a grip on the handle and gave it a good yank.

The door didn't budge. I tried again and felt the slightest bit of give. The paint had sunk into the crack that marked the edge of the door, so I forced the screwdriver into the crack and worked it around the door, gouging out the paint. Soon I had a mess of paint chips on the floor. But I yanked again, and the door popped open.

The smell was terrible. Mildew and mold and long-ago dead things. I shone my flashlight into the darkness.

It was a small, shallow cellar—more of a crawlspace, really, carved into the surprisingly thick wall of the house. I had to step down into it, so I guess being a foot below ground level made it a "cellar." It was less than three feet wide and extended to my right. I stepped down and shined my light down the length of it. A shallow wine rack ran along the wall to the left. No bottles protruded from it. I moved the light to the right.

A deathly white man stood there in my light beam. He hissed at me.

I screamed.

He hissed.

I screamed with such force it was operatic.

He hissed back at me like a feral cat.

It was a good thing I went to the bathroom at the restaurant before leaving. I'm not quite old enough to need adult diapers, but I almost needed one today.

I stumbled backwards, hit my head on the stone wall, and felt my heart begin to explode.

"Sorry," the old man said. "Didn't mean to scare you. And the hissing was a reflexive action. To be honest, you scared me, too."

I uttered something that sounding like I was speaking in tongues at a church revival.

"I'm Roderick," he said. "But you can call me Rod."

I managed to keep myself from hyperventilating and sputtered the question of what he was doing there.

"I've been imprisoned here. What's your name?"

"For how long have you been here? How did you get food and water? And why didn't my realtor tell me about you? I thought sellers are legally required to reveal information like having an imprisoned man in the house."

"To answer your first question, I'm guessing I've been here at least a hundred years, but I don't know what year it is now. None of the owners knew I was here. As to the second question, I'm a vampire. I don't need food, except for, well, you know. I was essentially hibernating until you made all that noise and woke me up. How's my hair look? Do I have bed-head?"

He didn't have much hair. It was white and parted on one

side. He looked like he was in his early sixties. If he were a human, that is.

"Your hair is fine," I said.

"How kind of you to say. Now, I imagine you're wondering why a vampire with superhuman strength couldn't escape from this place?"

"Actually, I'm still trying to process the fact that a vampire is in the wine cellar of the inn I just bought."

"It's because of that." He pointed to the back of the door I had come through.

There was a flat, circular metallic object about the diameter of a drink coaster. It was silver, with stamped lettering in a language I didn't recognize running along the outer edge of its face. In the center was the shape of a dagger, with a narrow blade like an ice pick.

"Is that silver?" I asked.

"No. And vampires don't mind silver, despite what some silly movies say. That's just ridiculous. Werewolves, though, they're another story. Werewolves and silver don't mix."

"Okay. So what's the deal with this disk?"

"It contains magic that sealed me in this closet here by the order of the Clan of the Eternal Night, the vampire guild of San Marcos. The icon on it represents an assassination knife made for plunging into vampire hearts—"

"Wait," I said, trying to get Roderick back on track. I realized he hadn't spoken to anyone in over a hundred years, but I didn't have time for his rambling. "Why were you sealed in here?"

"Funny you ask, um, what did you say your name was? I remember now—you didn't say your name."

"I'm Darla. Now why were you sealed in the wall of my house?"

"It wasn't your house back then. It was actually my house.

Well, it was, until the bank took it from me. Unfairly, I might add. Banks were very unfair back then. I don't know if they're better now, but knowing banks, I doubt it."

"Let's get back on track, Roderick."

"You can call me Rod."

"Why were you sealed up in the wall of your house?" I asked with as forceful a voice I could muster after tearing vocal cords from my hysterical screaming a few moments ago.

"Why did the Vampire Guild punish me? The first reason is I was behind on my dues. Way behind. But, please, I was behind on my mortgage as well, and one needs to prioritize, doesn't one?"

"Go on."

"And there was the little misunderstanding."

"What do you mean?"

"All right, it was a very big misunderstanding. You see, Henry Flagler, the railroad magnate, had just connected San Marcos with his railroad, with which he transported very wealthy Northerners down here to stay in the very opulent hotels he was building. I turned my home into an inn to capitalize on that, to lure the travelers away from his hotels to my more intimate, luxury accommodations. That's what got me into trouble."

"You were sealed away in a wall for over a hundred years just for competing with Henry Flagler?"

"Ah, yes, in a way. Also, for luring his guests here and feeding on them."

"Okay. . ."

"The Vampire Guild is very strict about keeping our existence secret. Feeding on wealthy socialites from New York, Boston, and Chicago tends to bring unwanted attention from the newspapers."

"Okay."

"And the fact that my lodgings weren't exactly luxury didn't help. Although, I would have improved them if I hadn't been sealed away. And, you see, word spread that my little intimate inn was a dump. So they said. I found myself feeding on Flagler's guests on his own properties. That caused quite a public relations problem for us vampires."

"I can imagine. But let me get this straight," I said. "You're forbidden from feeding on the wealthy. Does that make it okay to feed on the poor?"

"No, not at all. This is not a social class issue. Well, the rich do eat well and have higher iron counts in their blood. But that was not the problem. I simply, well, I hate to admit it, but I lack the ability that most vampires have to mesmerize my prey. I can't make them forget I fed upon them. When you attack and feed upon people who have society reporters following them around constantly, it creates terrible publicity for vampires. Do you understand?"

I did. And all this talk about feeding was making me very nervous, being only a few feet away from this vampire in a tight space. I considered quickly escaping, nailing the door closed and letting him stay in here, sealed in by the strange metal disk.

But could I live here and run an inn knowing a vampire was sealed in the wall?

"How long could you remain in hibernation before you starved to death?" I asked anyway.

"I do not know. I hope you're not considering locking me up again."

"I hope you're not considering feeding on me," I said.

He laughed. "No. I'm considering if we can come to a mutually beneficial arrangement."

CHAPTER 7
COIN COLLECTOR

I drove to Mom's house as I considered my options. I now had an expensive mortgage on a nearly 300-year-old building that was probably several weeks away from bringing me any income. Said building was haunted, though I didn't know yet by how many ghosts, and if they were benign or malevolent. The fireplace in the front room had a talking gargoyle under the mantel —when he wasn't running off doing who knows what.

And to top it all off, there was a vampire in a hidden space in the wall. I had begun negotiations with this vampire to get him to leave the property, which he claimed his bank had unfairly taken from him. I had never met a vampire before, but I heard they can be extremely territorial.

My prospects for success with my business were fading fast. An inn that was haunted might seem colorful to some guests. An inn with a vampire was simply toxic. I was fairly certain that no insurance policy in the world would protect me from liability if guests were bitten by a vampire.

I had all that going for me. Assuming I didn't discover even more freaky facts about my new home.

I was looking forward to having some tea and then finding somewhere in my childhood home, away from Mom and Sophie and the customers, where I could read a book in peace. Preferably not in Mom's magic room in the turret where I had to sleep at night.

But life had other plans for me.

"I'm glad you're finally here," Mom said to me when I entered the back door into the kitchen. I had hoped by avoiding the front door, I would avoid scrutiny.

"I was checking on my new inn," I said.

"Oh, that's right. Congratulations. But listen dear, I have to check out some pieces I'm bidding on with an auction app. Sophie's at work, and I need you to watch the store while I'm gone."

"Are you serious? I'm exhausted." I realized I sounded like the sullen teenage I once was. The way my own daughter still talked to me sometimes.

"It's only two hours until closing time," Mom said. "But I'll be back sooner than that."

Before I could even agree, Mom grabbed her purse from the oven where she kept it during business hours, and was out the back door. Her old station wagon backed out of its space outside the detached garage and rolled past the kitchen windows to the street.

I decided to hide my purse in the oven, too. Then, I had just enough time to boil water and pour a cup of tea before the bell tinkled from someone entering the front door.

I wove a path through the forest of junk—sorry, antiques. I passed through what used to be the butler's pantry, the former dining room, and into the room previously known as the living room. This was where the jewelry display case and sales desk were.

A man bent over, studying the display case.

"Good afternoon," I said in the cheeriest voice I could muster.

He looked up at me as I slipped into the nook behind the display case and sales tables. My breath caught in my throat.

I didn't recognize the man, but somehow, I felt I knew him.

There was nothing distinct about him. He was somewhat tall and very thin. He wore a baseball cap and glasses. His khaki slacks were dirty, and his San Marco tourist T-shirt was brand new.

He looked up at me. His face was gaunt, and his nose showed signs of having been broken years ago. He smiled, revealing two missing teeth.

The memory appeared in my mind like a light switch turned on. My knees felt weak and the hairs on the back of my neck prickled.

"I'm interested in antique coins," he said. "Do you have any others besides the ones in this case?"

My heart was racing as I remembered my vision of Danielle's terrifying last moments.

"This is my mother's store," I said in a leaden voice. "But I believe these are the only coins she has."

He stood fully upright and moved closer to me with the case in between us.

"What about you? Do you have any coins?"

"No," I said, feeling my pockets for my cell phone. My heart sank when I remembered it was on the kitchen counter. "I don't collect coins."

"I think you do." His voice had lost all pretense of friendliness.

"You do? I didn't think I looked like the coin-collecting type," I said, forcing a joke.

"I know who you are," he said. His eyes bored into mine. "You were her friend. I saw you. You went to her store in the morning and found her body. I didn't mean to hurt her. But she lied to me. Don't lie to me, and you won't get hurt."

"But I—"

"Don't lie to me. You have the coin, don't you?"

"I don't know what you're talking about. I hadn't seen Danielle in a long time, and I don't know what coins she was selling. She sold a lot of old Spanish coins. Mom has two *reales* in the case here."

"I'm looking for a particular coin. I think you have it."

"How would you know what I have?" I asked, my fear making me angry. "You're paranoid. You think people have your coin and when they don't, you kill them. Are you going to kill everyone in San Marcos before you realize your stupid coin isn't here?"

I'm going to kill you, his voice rang out telepathically in my head.

He lunged at me. His torso hit the case, almost knocking it over, as he tried to grab me. I jerked backwards just in time to escape his hands.

And then I ran. This house was a maze, always shifting as the inventory changed, but I knew it better than any stranger would. I took off into the dining room with the man right behind me, but took a sharp turn between two armoires and slipped out into the central hallway.

A crash came from the dining room. I hoped it wasn't something expensive.

In Mom's house, even the hallway was a minefield of goods for sale. Which was fortunate for me, as the man tripped on a metal watering can behind me.

I went into the front parlor on the opposite side of the house, trying to formulate a plan of how to survive this. I was just trying to escape the killer without allowing myself to get trapped in a room I couldn't get out of. I also needed a defensive weapon. Well, a better one than the old tennis racquet I grabbed just now.

The killer was in the room. I went behind shelves filled with lava lamps. Where did Mom find thirty lava lamps? And *why*?

A gun fired, and a lava lamp exploded two feet away from me. I didn't realize he was armed. This was very, very bad.

I ducked behind a wooden horse from a merry-go-round. Another shot rang out and the poor horse took a bullet for me.

"How will killing me help you find a coin?" I shouted, probably unwisely.

She can identify me. She has to die. Then I search her purse and any safes I find.

My telepathy is spotty and definitely does not work on demand. And it wasn't telling me anything I didn't already know right now.

I slipped into the study, which, appropriately, contained used books. But there was also a headless mannequin, a pogo stick, and a table with Tiffany lamps.

And paperweights. I threw a heavy brass fish at the killer when he appeared in the doorway. It hit him in the chest, and I didn't stick around to see if it did any harm. I escaped into the hallway and then back into the living room.

I was running out of places to run on the ground floor. I didn't want to go upstairs where I'd be trapped. I needed to get outside, but couldn't go out the back door because I didn't want him in the kitchen where my purse, holding the coin, was.

Footsteps came from the dining room, so I sprinted out into the hallway headed for the front door. I glanced behind me, saw him in the rear of the hallway aiming his gun at me, and dove into the front sitting room right before the bullet hit the front door.

The windows were all locked for security, not to mention

probably stuck from swelled wooden sashes. This was not working out well.

I tried to read his thoughts, but nothing came into my head. His footsteps creaked along the wooden floor toward me. He was passing through the study to reach this room.

I retreated into the hallway and tried to make it out the front door again. But through the sidelight windows, I saw Sophie coming up the front walk.

If I went out there, we both would get shot.

Instead, I bolted up the stairs to the second floor. The back bedroom had a balcony, and I was willing to chance jumping one story to the ground.

The problem was the stairs were noisy. And I was a sitting duck on the way up. But somehow, I made it to the top without getting shot. I rounded the corner at the landing while his feet pounded up the steps.

There was a box of books on the landing. I leaned over the railing and dropped the box. It hit him squarely on the head. He crashed headfirst onto the stairs. He groaned and tried to get to his feet. Also on the landing was an assortment of water skis and random sports gear leaning against the wall. I grabbed an old wooden baseball bat.

It was time to make my jump, but I had to warn Sophie somehow. Again, I remembered my phone was in the kitchen. So I ran to the bedroom on the front of the house and tried to open the window. Sure enough, it was stuck.

The room was filled with mirrors hanging on the walls, and wardrobe mirrors crowding the floor. I used the baseball bat to poke through a bottom pane of the window.

"Sophie, don't go inside," I screamed through the hole.

She was right below me, just about to mount the steps to the front porch.

"There's a man with a gun in here," I shouted to her. "Call nine-one-one."

The floorboards groaned in the hallway just outside the room.

I was trapped in here, just like I had tried to avoid.

I hid behind one large standing mirror. But, out of the corner of my eye, I saw my reflection in another standing mirror to my left. And that, in turn, was reflected in the ones across from it. Mirrors on the wall picked up the reflections from those mirrors, which then reflected into others.

When the killer walked into the room, he must have seen a dozen or more Darlas in here. I could see his reflection, too, a confused expression on his face.

Which friggin' mirror is she behind? said his thoughts in my head.

He walked further into the room, looking behind each mirror he passed. Now he was close enough I could smell his rank sweat.

The tips of his shoes appeared, just visible past the edge of my mirror hiding place.

I tightened my grip on the baseball bat. And the slight movement, reflected in dozens of mirrors, caught his eye.

But he turned his head in the wrong direction, toward the mirrors to my left.

I quickly stepped around the right side of my mirror. He and I both saw me raise my bat in all the mirrors. But my swing was faster than he could figure out which direction to turn.

The sound of the bat hitting his head wasn't the crack of a home run. It was more like a watermelon smashed on the floor.

He dropped to the ground. I resisted the urge to smash his skull into pulp, and ran out the room, down the stairs, and outside.

Sophie was talking to the neighbor next door. I ran toward them.

"Don't stand out here!" I yelled breathlessly. "He could come out any moment."

We scurried onto the neighbor's porch just as three police cars with flashing lights pulled up in front of Mom's house.

"He's in the second-floor front bedroom," I shouted to them.

Unless I didn't bonk him hard enough. In that case, he could be anywhere.

Not long after the three officers went inside, a Fire Rescue ambulance rolled up to the house. Now I worried I had bonked him too hard. But about twenty minutes later, the paramedics rolled out a stretcher accompanied by an officer.

The killer lay atop it with his hands in cuffs.

While a different officer, an African-American woman, interviewed me on the neighbor's porch, Detective Samson showed up. I had to repeat the entire story again for him.

"Do you believe this individual is the person whose memory you 'read' after the murder?" he asked.

"Yes."

"Why do you believe that?"

I couldn't tell him about taking the coin and Danielle's memory that I read from it. I would have to bend the truth a little.

"I recognized him. When I described to you the impressions of the killer I got from the bronze angel, I didn't remember until now him seeing his reflection in some glass at the gallery. When I saw him today, I realized I recognized him."

Samson nodded. I think he believed me, at least as far as he could believe anything about psychometry.

"Why did he show up here today?" he asked.

"He claimed I had something of Danielle's that he wanted. I didn't know what he was talking about."

"Do you have reason to believe he saw you at the crime scene?"

"I do now," I said. "I showed up at the gallery many hours after the murder, but he must have come back to watch the place. And he must have been following me since then. That really freaks me out."

"It happens sometimes," Samson said. "That's why I had told you to watch your back."

"Do you think this guy was hired to steal whatever it was he was trying to steal? He doesn't seem like the type to be interested in a rare coin."

I had read in his thoughts something about powerful forces sending him on his mission.

"He used a fake identity to book the motel room. But we ran the prints we found in the room and ID'd him. He has a record of small-time felonies. So, yes, I think someone hired him."

"So even with the murderer in custody, I'm still not safe? Is that the case? I mean, whoever hired him still wants the coin or whatever he was after."

"That's a possibility," Samson said. "Let me know if you notice anything suspicious. We'll keep you out of harm's way."

After he left, I kind of wished he had said something more like he'd personally see to my safety. Or lay down his life to save mine. Or—oh, never mind.

When I went inside Mom's house, Sophie was waiting for me at the customer counter.

"How are you going to explain this to Grammers?" she asked, as if I was a teenager who had violated my curfew.

"I'll explain it the same way I did to you."

"Yeah, but she's gonna freak out."

"She's been robbed here once before. She knocked the guy out with a sleep spell. Your grandmother is a tough cookie."

"When she's the one in danger. Not when it was her daughter. And, almost, me. And not when there are bullet holes all over the place."

"Not all over the place. As I recall, he fired three times. The only loss was a lava lamp, so it wasn't truly a loss in my opinion."

"Still, she's going to freak out. You know it."

Yeah, I knew it. I wish she'd come home already so I could get it over with. It was so odd that I was going to be scolded for irresponsible behavior by my mother—in front of my daughter.

Our eyes snapped to the side windows as the rumble of Mom's old station wagon moved down the driveway next to the house, parking in front of the detached garage. Sophie and I glanced at each other like co-conspirators about to face the music. When the door of the car slammed shut, we rushed into the kitchen, and I realized no one had done anything about preparing dinner.

The back door opened, and Mom came in.

"I purchased the piece for a wonderful price, and I need some help to carry it inside." She stopped a few paces from the door. Her nostrils flared and her head swiveled.

"What was going on here?" she asked.

"Um, nothing much," I said, before realizing I sounded like Sophie had when she was fourteen.

"Evil has been in this house," Mom said.

"You're darn right!" Sophie exclaimed.

I gave her a side-wise glare.

Mom marched past us and out of the kitchen. We scurried after her.

She stood beside the display case that was knocked off kilter.

"What happened here? No, don't answer. I don't want to hear any nonsense."

She exited the living room into the central hallway.

"Bullet hole in the front door. From the inside. Don't try to convince me it was a drive-by shooting."

I was going to say that it didn't require her supernatural powers to diagnose the bullet hole since the police had helpfully marked it with an orange sticker. But I held my words.

She crossed the hallway into the sitting room.

"What happened to my lava lamp?"

"You have plenty of them, Mom," I said.

"And a bullet hole in the wall behind it, And one in my horse—oh, bless my soul."

"It's made of wood. It won't die, Mom. Let's move on."

I prayed she wouldn't go to the second floor where there was blood in the front bedroom.

"Is this related to your friend's murder?" she asked me.

I nodded.

She nodded in return and ruminated for an excruciatingly long time.

"Has the Memory Guild contacted you yet?" she asked.

"Not officially. I met a, well, a gargoyle who said I should join. But no one has told me how."

"What we need to do then is hire them. To find out what the deal is with that coin of yours."

"Mom! What are you talking about?"

"You're not the only one with telepathic abilities," she said.

This was news to me. But it explained a lot. Like why I was grounded, when I was a kid, more than anyone I knew.

CHAPTER 8
LONG STRANGE TRIP

I stood in the front room of my inn. Or I should say, soon-to-be-open inn. *Hopefully*, soon to be. Anyway, I stared at the gigantic fireplace with its imposing mantel and stonework from Medieval England. Specifically, I studied the four ornamental stone gargoyles that helped support the shelf of the mantel, hoping the one of the far left would come to life, so I could talk to it.

A week ago I couldn't have imagined such an absurd scenario. But here I was.

"Archibald, we need to talk."

The gargoyle remained how gargoyles are supposed to remain: as inanimate stone. Archibald's head was the size of a cantaloupe, framed by the front portions of wings and resting on claw-like hands. He looked demonic, which was typical of gargoyles, or grotesques, since they were meant to scare away evil spirits.

You could describe him as a cross between a flying monkey from *The Wizard of Oz* and an iguana in a foul mood. He sneered with a human-like tongue hanging out. The grayish stone of which he'd been carved was slightly darkened by soot beneath his chin. His appearance didn't match at all the friendly personality Archibald had displayed.

But today, he wasn't cooperating.

I had set up an account with the electrical utility, but this morning, the sun flooding the tall windows bathed the room in a warm, peaceful hue that made the centuries-old room look like a Renaissance-era painting. That was perfectly appropriate. When I had walked up to the entrance of the home across the cobblestone street and breathed in the tang of the saltwater-laced air while seagulls flew above, I imagined I was back in the earliest days of San Marcos. Layers of history are under the surface of everything in this town once you scratch it.

"Archibald, please. I have a question to ask you." My voice echoed in the room, sparsely furnished and with a high ceiling. Ceilings this tall were rare in Spanish Colonial-era homes.

I knew nothing about gargoyles. Especially not that some were supernatural and could speak and move around. I didn't know what special powers they had. Most of all, I didn't know how to get them to talk to you.

I reached out and touched him on his nose. He felt like a cool, lifeless stone. I couldn't think of anything else to do, so I cupped his face and head with both my hands. Maybe my body heat would activate him. Or we could establish some sort of psychic connection.

I stood there with my hands on him for a long time. I was feeling stupid, as well as hungry. My lower back was becoming increasingly sore. At my age, everything in my body was beginning to go bad. My lumbar discs had been among the first to do so.

My stomach growled loudly, since I hadn't eaten breakfast today. It was a long, rumbling, gurgling song of anguish that echoed in the empty room.

My hands tingled as the stone beneath them vibrated. Then loud laughter broke out.

I stepped away from the mantel. The gargoyle had come alive. The face, while still made of stone, had become fully animated with an amused smile as laughter poured from it.

"Archibald! You're back."

"I didn't go anywhere," he said. "I was sleeping. That's what gargoyles do most of the time."

"What did I do to wake you up? Was it the warmth of my skin? My psychic energy?"

"It was the hilarious sound your stomach made," he said.

"Oh. I see."

"So, what can I do for you, Miss Darla?" he asked.

"When we met, you said I should join the Memory Guild. Well, I'm ready now. How do I sign up?"

"It's good to hear that you are willing. But as far as being ready, that's up to the Guild to decide. When we ascertain your paranormal or supernatural powers are sufficiently strong, and your control of them is thorough, then we will come for you."

"Oh. When do you think I'll be ready?" I asked.

"I'm not on the membership committee, dear. But I'm confident they will come for you not a moment too soon or too tardy."

"I can't afford to wait. How about if I hire the Guild?"

"Why would you do that?"

"I have a mystery to solve. Don't you solve mysteries for clients?"

"Occasionally, to bring in revenue. You see, our mission to be the guardians of memory and history is pretty much a charity. What kind of mystery do you want us to solve? We don't investigate cheating spouses or crooked business partners. We're not a detective agency."

"It's about an ancient coin that someone is desperate to get ahold of. My friend was murdered because of this coin. I've only begun to read the memories in the coin, and I'm certain it has been in San Marcos since the city's earliest days."

"What exactly do you want the Guild to solve?"

"I want to know, why is the coin so special? And who is trying so hard to get it? This person directed the killer who murdered Danielle and almost killed me yesterday. My life will continue to be in danger because of this coin. Even if I get rid of it, they won't believe I don't have it."

"I see. The Guild might take on your assignment. I will fill them in, and if they're interested, they will contact you."

"Thank you. I appreciate it."

"It was nice speaking with you, Miss Darla. I shall return to sleep now."

"Wait, I have a question for you: where were you yesterday? You were missing from the mantel."

"As a gargoyle, I prefer that my private life stay private. When you spend hundreds of years out in the open, exposed to human eyes, you need a little privacy sometimes."

"Okay. Sorry."

"Cheers," he said. And with that, he stuck his tongue out and became once again simple, inanimate stone.

I had so much work to do on the house, I didn't know where to start. But all this talk of the coin reminded me of how little time I spent reading the memories that clung to it.

Since I was alone in the house here—except for the gargoyle, vampire, and ghosts—I decided to read the coin again.

After the attack at Mom's house, I had left the coin in the cellar with Roderick guarding it. My agreement with him was he could live there for the time being, as long as he promised not to hunt any humans on the property or the neighborhood. I removed the seal from the inside of the cellar door and placed it on the outside door of the cottage where I'd be living to protect me when I moved in.

Once guests began staying here, we would review our agreement. If he even tried to feed on a guest, or even scare one, I would kick him out immediately. How one kicks out a vampire, I wasn't quite sure. Especially one who once owned the property and seemed to believe he could challenge his foreclosure and eviction from over a hundred years ago.

In the meantime, a vampire seemed like the perfect guard for the coin, as long as he was more aggressive with intruders than he was with me. But I gave him a pass, because no one had opened that door in over a century.

But I needed to open it today.

"Knock-knock. Wakey, wakey," I said in my best mommy voice before opening the door.

Roderick crawled off the shelf in the wine rack, blinking his eyes, though very little light from the kitchen seeped into this crypt.

I smiled at the sleepy vampire. "Sorry, do you mind if I—"

"I refuse to guard your coin if you're going to pop in on me every time you get the urge to fondle it."

"Please," I said. "I need to, just this time."

He sighed theatrically. And then retrieved it from the inside breast pocket of his decaying suit jacket. He handed it to me.

Instantly, I felt the power surging in this tiny disk of metal. My hand was shaking from the vibration.

"Thanks! Go back to bed, sleepyhead!"

I closed the door, rolled the refrigerator back in front of it, and then my legs gave out as a trance came over me. I dropped to my butt on the floor, leaning my back against the fridge.

My palm was burning from the coin, but I nevertheless closed it tight. And I—

—*see the glitter of something fall from the Huguenot's hand as the blood pools beneath his neck before it soaks into the sand. There are red patches of sand all across this area of the dunes. Soon, the entire area will be crimson. I hold the object in my hand, a gold coin with Aztec markings. Why would the Frenchman be carrying this? And in its center is—*

(Flash of light)

—as a priest, I am not used to receiving gifts from dying men after I have already absolved them. Maybe before, but not after. But he wanted me to have this coin that came in a small wooden box with a note written in his barely literate hand. If only I hadn't waited so long to read the note. If only—

(Flash)

—I run with everything in me, as the night watchman in the museum blows his whistle and runs after me. I sure as heck hope I stole something worthwhile. But I—

(Flash)

—didn't expect to find something like this in a pawn shop. It has to be worth more than the owner realizes. I should try to see what I could get for it from a coin dealer. I wonder—

(Flash)

—I pray to you, God, to save me. I don't have my crucifix. Is this coin enough to show my devotion? The mast has just broken in the storm and we're going to founder unless you, in your infinite mercy, intercede and save us. Please, almighty Lord, please. Water is rushing into the cabin. Oh, it—

(Flash)

—well, I'll be danged! The way the detector was pinging, I thought it was a nail, but look here: I've found myself an actual Spanish treasure coin! Nearly ten years of beachcombing and I finally win the ultimate prize. Boy, it's heavy—

I dropped the coin and finally snapped out of the visions. It felt as if I had been randomly skipping among those who had possessed the coin in its long history. I had the sense that there were hundreds more memories clinging to the coin, and I simply couldn't take experiencing more of them. Some were mundane, but the terror of the person about to die at sea was too intense to bear.

This new gift of mine, psychometry, was truly powerful. But it would not do me any good if it continued to be so random. I needed to learn how to control it.

I suspected it could also be dangerous if I wasn't careful. I worried I could act out the scenarios I was experiencing and accidentally hurt myself. But the real danger was psychological trauma. If I had to experience Danielle's death again, and if it was more intense than last time, I could become really messed up.

I found the coin on the floor beside my leg and stood up. It was more of an operation than it should have been, my fifty-year-old bones and muscles and lumbar discs protesting bitterly.

I didn't feel like moving the fridge and waking Roderick to return the coin to his care. So I placed it beneath all the junk in my purse.

"Yes, you will need that."

My head swiveled, searching for the source of the voice. It sounded like Archibald's.

"Right here," he said.

His upper torso was attached to the subway tile above the range, just below the exhaust hood. I wondered if he had more than a head, wings, and arms and, if not, how he managed to leave the house.

"How did you get there?"

"That's a gargoyle secret I'll share another time," he said.

"I have to admit you look pretty good on that wall, like you've always been there. Maybe you'd like it here better, away from your three brothers who don't talk."

"I would prefer not to be splattered with hot cooking oil."

"Good point," I said.

"I'm here to give you the news. The Guild is ready to meet you."

"That's excellent," I said, beaming. "When do they want to do it?"

"Time is relative to the Guild. Some of us have been around for hundreds of years, you see. It matters not to us if you meet us in five minutes or five years."

"Well, I would prefer five minutes. But I don't think I could get there that fast. Where are they located?"

Archibald laughed. The gargoyle had a nasty, coughing sort of laugh.

"We don't have a clubhouse or an office with a water cooler and conference rooms. We're located . . . everywhere."

"I don't think that will work with my mapping app. Can you be more specific?"

He spread his little arms wide. "We work within the history and memories of San Marcos."

"You're not being helpful."

He laughed again. "Stay where you are. I will lead you to the meeting."

The moment his words left the air, I was gone, too. It wasn't like psychometry, where I disappeared into someone else's consciousness. In this case, I was still me. But I wasn't in my house anymore.

The problem was, I didn't know where I'd gone. I floated in darkness and emptiness.

"Come right along with me," Archibald said from the darkness.

Suddenly, I was gliding above the beach as if I was parasailing. But nothing was holding me up. I was flying by my own power southward at the edge of the surf, the ocean to my left and land to my right. Instead of being frightened, I enjoyed it. I felt like I was dreaming and knew I wouldn't be hurt.

"Um, Archibald," I said, though my voice resonated in my head, not in my throat. "Are you sure this is safe?"

"Your body is still in your kitchen," he said. "Only your mind and spirit are flying."

I recognized the occasional formations of coquina rocks from our city's beaches. But there were no homes or condos anywhere. No people, either. Just seagulls, terns, and pelicans.

I rather liked the beach this way.

"All right, time to take a right," Archibald said in my head.

I banked gracefully to the right, over the dunes covered with sea oats, over palm trees, marshes, mangroves, forests of oak and pine. There wasn't a single sign of human habitation.

Suddenly, a dark cloud, solid and abrupt as a wall from the ground to the sky, was in front of me. I wasn't sure I wanted to fly into it.

"Keep going," Archibald said. "It's safe. I'm still here beside you."

I couldn't see him, though.

When I broke through the wall of the cloud, the landscape became a hellscape. Fire and molten lava flowed through jagged shards of rock. It was either Hell literally, or the planet in its infancy before it cooled.

"It's not Hell," Archibald said. "But don't look down. Keep your eyes on the horizon."

I tried to, but didn't see any horizon. There was just darkness and a red-orange glow.

Then, as if in a dream, everything changed. I stood on the barest hint of a trail in a jungle, thick with lush tropical plants. Ferns as tall as I, palm fronds broader than a house, twisting vines, and thick tree trunks that rose so high they disappeared into the mist. The sound of buzzing insects and chirping birds was almost deafening, along with strange hoots and screeches from creatures I couldn't imagine.

I didn't recognize the type of forest I was in. It must have been from an ancient time.

"Keep moving," Archibald said. "Follow the trail."

It wasn't a human trail, but one made by animals' repeated passage through the plants on the forest floor. But I followed it as it wound between the giant trees. My vision was clear, my hearing sensitive, but my sense of smell and touch weren't there. I didn't feel my feet hitting the ground. But that's the way it often was in dreams.

Ahead of me was a natural tunnel formed by saplings bending inward, a dark shady corridor. The trail ran toward a giant tree trunk with an opening. I had to bend slightly as I entered the corridor.

Then, before my eyes, the walls of this tunnel of trees turned into stone. It was the porous limestone of underground Florida, craggy, full of nooks and crannies and pockets eroded by ancient seas.

But humans had been in here, boring this shaft through the rock. I saw the indications of tools carving the stone. The floor had been worn smooth. And my path was illuminated by natural sconces in the walls of the tunnel where crude oil lamps burned. This was the first sign of human presence since my astral journey had begun.

After a while of walking through the twisting tunnel, rising and falling gently in elevation, I saw brighter light ahead.

The walls and ceiling widened, and soon I was in a large, round cavern. The walls were large blocks of stone; the roof was a giant dome lined with brick. Torches burned from brackets along the walls below the point where the dome curved inwards.

The room was empty.

"Welcome to the Memory Guild," Archibald said, his gargoyle head, wings, and arms mounted to the stone wall above me.

CHAPTER 9
THE MEMORY GUILD

At first, I was alone in the domed room except for Archibald. But then, in a blink of my eyes, people stood in front of me, one woman sitting in a wheelchair. I counted eight individuals, including Archibald.

"You are Darla Chesswick?" asked the oldest person there. He was tall with long white hair and a giant white beard. He wore a blue suit without a tie. There was something biblical about him.

"Yes, I'm Darla."

"Welcome to the Guild. I'm Dr. Sven Noordlun, the administrator. I'm the chair of the history department at San Marcos College."

"Pleased to meet you," I said.

"You already know Archibald," he said. "The rest of you please introduce yourselves."

"I'm Laurel," said the woman in the wheelchair who looked around my age. "I'm a psychometrist like yourself."

"I'm Diego," said a medium-height man of African descent.

"I've been in San Marcos for nearly five hundred years. Yes, I'm a vampire."

"I'm James," said a burly guy with unruly brown hair and beard. I recognized him as a blacksmith in the historical reenactment village for tourists. "I'm a metal-speaker. I can communicate with the iron, steel, and precious metals of our city."

"I'm Summer," said a beautiful, wispy young woman with Elven features and blond hair. "I'm a wood-speaker. I communicate with the manmade wooden structures in town, and with trees and more advanced plants."

"I'm Gloria, I'm a psychic," said a petite older woman with short silver hair. "Your garden variety, Tarot-card and palm-reading psychic. But I can see the past as well as the future. Pleased to meet you and your destiny."

"I'm Diana," said a stout, middle-aged woman with jet-black hair. Was it dyed? "I'm an astral witch. I specialize in astral travel through space and time."

"She's the one who made it possible for you to travel here today," Sven explained.

"My name is Sage," came a voice, followed by a figure materializing out of thin air. She was an older woman, hippie-like. "I'm the liaison to the spiritual world. I can communicate with spirits of those who have passed."

"Sage is a ghost," Sven said.

"I'm not a ghost," Sage insisted.

"She's a ghost who can't admit it to herself," Sven said with a big smile.

Sage frowned and disappeared.

"If you ever need to contact Sage, I can do it for you," Gloria said. "I'm a medium, too."

"So there you have it," Sven said. "We are the core members of the Memory Guild, though we often work with other individuals on a project basis. We're assembling here today in this virtual manner for secrecy and convenience. It's rather like a video conference without the internet frustrations. But we also meet in person, when needed. I suspect you'll be working with Laurel frequently. Particularly regarding this coin you've found."

"Um, how much do you charge for helping me with this mystery?" I asked, inwardly cringing from having to bring this up. But, let's face it, I was short on cash because of all the money I needed to sink into the inn.

"We decided we won't take you on as a client," Sven said. "Instead, we're granting you an internship with the Guild, since your case is so interesting, and we've done a better assessment of your abilities."

"Wow, thank you. That is very kind of you. But how can you assess my abilities? I've only just met you."

"You won't understand now, but will in time. As the guardians of memory and history, we can sense when there is unusual activity. To use an analogy, we can hear when the books are moved about in the bookcase."

"You mean, you sensed it when I read the memories from the coin?"

"In a manner, yes."

"Wow," I said. "That's kind of freaky."

"You must understand," Diego the vampire said, "your readings were harmless. Beneficial, actually, in preserving memories. But there are those who seek to destroy memory, or alter it maliciously, in order to rewrite history. We have to be on alert to stop that."

I nodded. I understood what the Guild did a little better now. But just a little.

"So, while we help you discover the story behind this coin and those who seek to possess it, you will be training. Improving your abilities and learning what we do here. As an intern, you will take on such assignments as we see fit to give you."

"Sounds great! I'm ready," I said with a smile. Which quickly faded when I saw by their expressions that I was acting too stupidly enthusiastic.

Sven, with eyebrow raised, said, "Your assignments are as follows: meet with Laurel tonight for a reading session of the coin."

"Sounds good," I said. "I'm free all evening."

"In addition, you will use your ability to discover who has been vandalizing the Huguenot Cemetery recently. Headstones have been smashed and defaced. We consider it a cardinal sin to damage the records of births and deaths and the names of those who have passed. Official records were not thorough during the time when most of the cemetery's inhabitants were buried. Headstones are all we have for several of them."

"Oh. I see. How, exactly, am I supposed to find out who the vandals are?"

Sven exchanged a disappointed look with Laurel.

"Wait!" I said. "I'll touch the damaged headstones, of course. But in case they used sledgehammers and never touched the headstones directly, I'll also touch every bit of the fence they climbed over. There has to be something they laid hands on."

The barest hint of a smile appeared on Sven, if you could make it out beneath his bushy mustache and beard.

"Um, how do I keep from being arrested for trespassing?"

"The cemetery is open during the daytime, silly," Laurel said, grinning.

"Oh. Right. Of course." Then, I remembered something. "Psychometry put me in the mind of my friend's murderer. But I couldn't learn his name. His name didn't enter his mind at the time. The same will probably be the case of the vandals."

"That happens all the time," Laurel said. "There are ways to complete the puzzle and identify them. The Guild and I will help you."

"Ladies and gentlemen, this concludes this special meeting of the Memory Guild of San Marcos," Sven said. "Until we meet again."

He clapped his hands, and the world went dark.

Soon, I saw starlight and, as my eyes adjusted, I made out the silhouettes of low buildings around me. I stood on a cobblestone street. The neighborhood was familiar; I was near the inn. But something was off. The uniform darkness was unnatural for the city. I walked past a house that was close to the street and saw a candle burning inside the window. Up ahead, at the street corner, in a lamp attached to a building, a flame burned oil. There were no wires or cables anywhere. No fire hydrants. No utility boxes on the sides of buildings.

I was in an era long before mine.

A throng of angry voices echoed down the street behind me, growing louder as the crowd approached. As it drew closer, I heard crying, as well. I stepped into a narrow alley far from any light.

Soon, a handful of soldiers wearing metal helmets and breast plates marched past the alley. They pulled a woman in a night-dress, her hands bound before her with rope. She sobbed hysterically. Right behind her was a group of civilian men and women shouting insults at her. I heard the word *bruja* several times. Witch. Behind them came a small group of anguished women insisting on the prisoner's innocence.

"This is but one of the things the Guild fights against," said Archibald's voice behind me. I could barely make him out in the darkness attached to a wall. "Rumors, lies, and conspiracy theories create injustices like witch hunts with needless suffering and harm. Then lies cover up what happened. The innocent shall not suffer in vain, and the ignorant shall not triumph. That is, if we do our jobs."

"Is this scene real?" I asked.

"Yes. The year is sixteen twelve. The woman you just saw was imprisoned, accused of witchcraft, and died in captivity. Go now, follow them."

"Follow the mob?"

"Yes. Hurry!"

I left my hiding spot and hurried down the street until I saw stragglers from the mob ahead of me crossing a small square. As I got closer, it became easier to see.

There was a lamppost up ahead with an electric bulb. One thing about living in an ancient city, certain blocks look the same for hundreds of years. But there was no mistaking the clues of modernity: trash cans, telephone lines. I passed a vintage soda pop sign and then a car parked behind a house, a Model A Ford.

I caught up to the mob. They weren't in Renaissance garb anymore. But it wasn't quite modern either. Men wore suspenders and hats. The women wore dresses that hung to their ankles. I wondered if the Ford I'd seen was actually a current model.

We were in a poorer residential neighborhood now, with oak trees and more 1920s cars. The mob was in front of a house, and a fight broke out. Soon, the people streamed toward me.

And instead of a frightened woman, a black man was in their clutches. His shirt was torn and his face bloody. He was barely conscious, and the men dragged more than led him.

The faces in the mob contorted with vicious hatred.

They were coming right at me. But instead of moving aside, I stood my ground.

"What you are doing is wrong," I shouted.

They didn't hear me, nor see me. They walked right around me, like water swirling past a channel marker.

Of course. I wasn't really here. Is this how it feels to be a ghost? I wondered.

Unsure of what to do, I followed the mob. But, it soon

became clear that they were not going to the police station. They crossed a wide street that was devoid of traffic at this hour. Based on the position of the moon, I guessed it was still hours before dawn.

The mob entered a park, one I didn't recognize, as I realized I was in a part of town unfamiliar to me. Yes, unfamiliar because I was a white girl, and this was where the African-Americans lived.

There were other people waiting in the park who grew excited as the mob and its prisoner arrived.

Then, I saw the rope draped over a tall limb of the tree.

I screamed and waved my arms, but no one noticed me, of course. How could I stop this? I couldn't. This was a scene from history playing in front of me like a video.

I refused to watch it.

"Archibald, help me!"

"Lies, rumors, conspiracy theories," he whispered in my ear. "Breeding hatred and ignorance. Harming the innocent. Emboldening the wicked. This is what we must fight. And the fight will never end, because of the weakness inherent in human minds."

"I understand," I said. "Now, can we get out of here?"

"Of course," Archibald said from the wall of my kitchen as I sat on the floor against the fridge. "But we can never truly leave."

I looked around to reassure myself that I was still in my kitchen, bright with sunlight streaming in the window and the fluorescent lights on the ceiling.

"I really need to get rid of those lights," I said aloud.

When I looked at the wall again, Archibald was gone.

I willed my middle-aged body to its feet and went into the front room. Archibald was back in place beneath the fireplace mantel. He was, once again, unmoving insentient stone.

My watch said it was only a few minutes after I had finished reading the coin and Archibald had first appeared on the kitchen wall.

The disturbing scenes I had just witnessed weighed on my mind. But I had a heavy load of weight there already. I now had an assignment to check out the cemetery. And that was in addition to all the work I needed to do to my new home to get it up and running as an inn.

I'll be perfectly honest and admit that I'm the most disorganized person ever. I'm bad about making lists and even worse about following them. I'm impulsive and easily distracted. This place would never be operational unless I got my act together. I had to focus on the most critical needs first. The cosmetic improvements could wait.

I had an old-school clipboard holding a legal pad. A sharpened Number Two pencil. And a roll of measuring tape. Time to get this sorted out.

Many of the rooms were furnished, thank God, and many of the furnishings were nice antiques. But a few pieces needed replacing. In some rooms, there were missing items. I went from room to room, making notes of any damages that needed repair.

I had to buy all new linens and pillows, towels, shower curtains, some new drapes—the list was endless. A few rooms needed touch-up paint.

On the third floor, I avoided touching the doorknob of the room where something horrible had happened. I'd had enough drama today already. As I was about to head back downstairs, something caught my eye.

The trapdoor to an attic, on the ceiling of the hallway.

I was absolutely certain it had not been there when I was here last. I had specifically looked for an attic and hadn't seen this door. Who could miss it? It was right there on the ceiling. Was I nuts?

An eyebolt protruded from the door. There should be a pole with a hook on it that allowed you to pull open the trapdoor and lower the folded stairs.

But where was the pole? I didn't really have time to look everywhere, but I was very curious about what was in the attic. In a historic home like this, there could be incredible finds squirreled away up there.

I looked in the linen closet off the hallway. No pole. I checked the closets of each of the bedrooms on this floor. No pole.

I went downstairs and looked in the closet under the stairs. It wasn't there, nor was it in any of the storage closets I opened. I wasn't in the mood to search the entire property for this pole, so I grabbed a stepladder and brought it upstairs.

Only to find the trapdoor wasn't there anymore.

Was I going insane? It had been right there, right above me, just minutes ago. I climbed the ladder and ran my hands along the ceiling. It was perfectly smooth. No seams or edges.

Was I simply disoriented? I moved the ladder around the hallway and felt the ceiling along the way. Nope, the trapdoor simply wasn't here.

When I had noticed its existence today, I assumed I had missed it before, not having been sufficiently observant. But now I wondered if something supernatural was going on.

I went down to the front room to ask Archibald if he knew anything about it. But he was in his stone state and neither touching him nor speaking to him woke him up.

I had to get out of here right now. Wouldn't a trip to the cemetery be a pleasant diversion?

CHAPTER 10
FACE TIME

Dennis lay awake on the bottom bunk. It was around 4:00 a.m., the only time the county jail was any degree of quiet, which still meant moans from nearby cells, ear-splitting snores, guys talking in their sleep. This was a time of terrible introspection, so Dennis tried to turn his thoughts away from himself and how he ended up in this cell, thanks to some fanatic with money to burn. When he was awake at this hour, he usually remembered tiny details that got lost during the day. He'd recall things he'd forgotten to do, or strange comments people had made—trivial stuff like that.

Right now, he wondered why his new cellmate had not left the upper bunk since he'd arrived yesterday afternoon. Not to eat, not to pee, not at all.

Dennis tried to listen for the guy's breathing, but heard nothing. It was none of his business, he told himself. The guy was pretty forgettable, a white dude named Carl who clearly didn't want to chitchat.

But it was really troubling Dennis that the guy was so inactive. Was something wrong with him? What if he was dead?

What if it turned out that he could have been saved if only Dennis had discovered something was wrong?

One key to surviving in jail was to mind your own business. Don't stick your nose into anything that didn't directly concern you.

But, really, this was too much.

"Hey, buddy," Dennis whispered. "You okay?"

No answer.

"Hey, let me know you're okay."

Still no answer. The guy was sleeping like a rock or was dead.

Dennis poked the bottom of the mattress above him. "Hey, you sick or something?"

Finally, he pushed firmly on the mattress, enough to wake anyone up. He felt the weight of Carl's body, but it didn't respond or move at all. The guy must be dead or in a coma.

Dennis got out of his bunk and stood next to the upper bunk. Carl lay on his side, facing the wall, his back to Dennis.

"Hey, Carl," Dennis said, his face close to the man's ear.

When Carl still didn't respond, Dennis reached out and grabbed his shoulder. He shook it gently. Then he pulled the unresponsive man onto his back. He pressed his fingers on the side of Carl's neck. The skin was cold and there was no pulse.

A bubble escaped from Carl's mouth.

And then, Carl turned his head and opened his eyes, which stared at Dennis blankly.

Dennis gasped in surprise. He stepped back from the bunk. But not far enough.

A snake head pushed out of Carl's mouth, followed by a second head, and then two more. The multi-headed serpent slid out, and five mouths filled with razor-sharp teeth opened.

And before Dennis could move, the hydra's mouths struck him on the face and neck, pulling him to the bunk as they did their grisly work.

Dennis didn't even get the chance to scream.

THE HUGUENOT CEMETERY WAS ON THE OTHER SIDE OF TOWN. I parked in a nearby tourist lot. Established in the early eighteen hundreds after Florida had been acquired by the United States, the cemetery held many of the protestants who had lived in this originally Catholic town.

When I realized how much wrought-iron fencing surrounded the property, my heart sank. It would take quite a long time to touch all of it, hoping to find the spot where the vandals had climbed over. Then there would be all the time needed to cover the desecrated graves. No wonder the intern got assigned this job.

I began at the southeastern corner and slowly worked my way along the eastern stretch of the fence. Tourists passing by, no doubt, wondered who that strange lady was holding onto the fence. Locals would think, "There's one of those wacky Chesswick women."

The fence was maybe six feet tall, with square vertical rods bisected by upper and lower crossbars. The rods ended at the top in decorative spikes protruding a few inches above the upper crossbar.

My job was made easier by my discovery that few people have touched the fence. After all, why would you? There was a lot of energy attached to the metal rungs of the eastern gate and the fence beside it. This was where people probably grabbed the metal to look inside the cemetery when the gate was locked. I didn't dwell here, because too many people had handled it. Maybe the vandals had, too, but their memories would be mixed in with the hundreds of others. I would wait to do a reading until I found a portion of the fence with significant energy.

I came across it halfway along the fence on the north side of the cemetery where there were several trees close to the gate providing cover for intruders.

Near the top of the fence, I began picking up significant energy from two, maybe three, people deposited there at the same time. I sensed nervousness, adrenaline, excitement. Also, anger and hatred. I couldn't get a fix on a single individual until I—

—am on God's mission to smite the heretics. They have always been heretics since the beginning, before their numbers grew so vast that they were unstoppable, like microbes spreading everywhere. We are here to spread a message, that is all. A message that few will understand. But those who do understand will be paralyzed with fear. Because they know I am not to be trifled with. Okay, now, up and over—

—I was clinging to the fence like it was the ledge of a tall building. I released the cast-iron rods, stepped back, and took a deep breath. Yeah, this was where the vandals climbed the fence. They basically had to hoist themselves up with upper body strength to get one foot on the upper cross bar and vault sideways over the spikes.

Someone was behind me. I whipped around.

It was Detective Samson.

"I saw you from the street and wondered what you were doing. I've been calling and texting you. I guess your phone is off."

It was. Cellphones and the supernatural don't mix.

"What do you need?" I asked.

"We need to talk. The man who assaulted you, Dennis Liszt, is dead."

I SAT WITH DETECTIVE SAMSON IN HIS CAR, PARKED ILLEGALLY next to the cemetery. The thought crossed my mind of how handsome he looked with his tanned face and neck against a white polo shirt with the San Marcos Police Department logo. As soon as I heard what he had to say, though, I forgot about his looks.

"His cellmate did what?" I asked.

"Ate his face. And neck," he added.

"And you say the cellmate is dead, too? Did he choke on his food?"

"We're waiting on toxicology reports, but I'm guessing the guy was on bath salts or something, like the guy who ate the homeless guy's face in Miami some years back. But what if it wasn't a random attack? That's what is bugging me. If it's true that someone hired Liszt to steal the item from your friend, maybe he wanted to silence Liszt. I just don't know how he could have arranged to get the assassin into the same cell in the county jail as Liszt. And how convenient is that to have the assassin die afterwards? This case is really bugging me."

It bugged me, too. With Liszt gone, I didn't know how Samson could discover who hired him. Maybe the secret could be found through the coin.

Or there might be a more direct route.

"Can I have access to Liszt's car?" I asked. "And any possessions that were in it?"

"Why?"

"I want to touch what he touched and read his memories. It might give some clues about who hired him."

"You're onto that psychic stuff again?"

"Yes, I am. And I found out your department sometimes uses psychics like me, so don't play dumb."

"I've never used them. I think it's a waste of time, unless

you've got a missing person case that's hit a dead end and you're desperate enough to listen to a cuckoo."

"Thank you for the compliment," I said.

"You know what I mean."

"Sadly, I do."

"C'mon, I wasn't trying to insult you."

"Maybe you weren't trying, but you succeeded."

"Okay, I'll look for the car at the impound lot and check the evidence locker for any possessions he may have had in it. Stop by the station tomorrow and I'll set you up."

I agreed, still pretending to be more offended than I actually was. We said goodbye, and I left his car and walked back to the cemetery fence.

"Hey, Ms. Chesswick," he called from his open window. "I forgot to ask. What are you doing with the fence?"

"Some desperate-cuckoo psychic work," I said and walked away.

When I reached the spot on the fence where I had been earlier, I moved my hands across the metal, trying to pick up the same memory I was reading before.

But I found a different one, from a different person. The wrought-iron railing hummed beneath my hand as I—

—helped the fat freak over the fence. Why was he even here with us tonight? Me and Beau could have done it ourselves. We don't need some out-of-shape, rich dude with us. The only exercise he gets is counting his money and flapping his jaws about his sacred mission to stop the people he doesn't like. I guess if you're rich, you can afford to cater to your paranoid conspiracy theories. Okay, my turn. Let him see how a fit person climbs over this—

—fence was warm beneath my hands. I let go.

Interesting, I thought. This obviously wasn't your run-of-the-mill vandalism. Did the Guild know that when they assigned this to me?

After probing the fence for several more minutes, I gave up. I couldn't find any more coherent memories, only fragmentary ones: random words and images. One of these guys was craving beer, but that didn't help me at all. It was time to examine the damaged headstones.

I walked back to the east gate and followed a brick pathway that passed through the center of the grounds. I soon spotted the desecrated graves to my right, cordoned off with yellow crime scene tape, not far from the fence where the vandals climbed over. Three headstones had been smashed to pieces with sledgehammers or something. The graves appeared to be from the same family based on what little I could read on the inscriptions on the pieces of broken stone. The one in the middle of the three had been a larger monument. An obelisk about six feet tall lay toppled on the grass. It had been perched upon a square base around four feet tall. The sledgehammers had worked on the base but hadn't destroyed it. The front of it which had held the inscriptions was smashed beyond recognition, though. I couldn't read anything. This person had suffered most of the desecrators' wrath.

I touched every inch of the stone, but picked up very little. They used sledgehammers, after all, not their hands. The toppled obelisk had traces of emotion attached to it. It was the thrill of pushing the heavy object to the ground. That was all.

I couldn't think of anything else to do here. But before I left, I searched the fragments of the other two headstones until I could piece together a last name.

Moulton.

It meant nothing to me, but that was what the internet was for. I returned to my car, turned my phone on, and searched "Moulton Huguenot Cemetery San Marcos."

I quickly found a website dedicated to historic graveyards in

Florida. It had a list of nearly 500 names of those buried here, including a Vincent Moulton, along with his wife and daughter.

And then it was back to searching. Vincent Moulton wasn't very famous, it seemed. A realtor in Milwaukee by the same name was dominating the search results. But finally, I found something.

Vincent Moulton, 1765-1840, was an academic and philosopher who spent the latter part of his life in San Marcos. What had he done to incur the wrath of these vandals? I supposed they could have chosen his family's graves at random, but based on the thoughts I read from the first vandal, Moulton meant something to him. He was trying to send a message. A message to whom was a good question, because clearly few people would know who the heck Vincent Moulton was.

I needed to do more research. There had to be a solution to this puzzle that would impress the Memory Guild and put me in their good graces.

I drove to Mom's where I'd use my laptop and her Wi-Fi to do a deeper search. I pulled into the driveway to leave room by the curb for customers. Her home was on a stretch of the street with several antiques dealers and thrift shops, so people often parked elsewhere and walked from shop to shop.

I went in through the kitchen, waved at Mom, and headed for the stairs. There were a good number of customers roaming the house. While I was in the hallway, I passed a customer studying the wooden horse. He seemed fixated with the bullet hole.

"Word is," I said to him, "a notorious mobster rode that horse on the merry-go-round when he was gunned down by the FBI."

He smiled at me. Maybe he even believed me.

I made it to the third floor and passed Sophie in the

bedroom she used. She was sitting on the bed, scrolling on her phone.

"Hi Sweetie," I said as I passed by.

I halted. What did I just see?

I retraced my steps to her room. She had dyed her black hair purple.

"Why did you do that?" I asked, trying to keep my voice friendly.

"What?"

"Your hair."

"I wanted to let a different side of me out," she said.

"Shouldn't you let the employable side of you out instead?"

"I have a job. The owner doesn't care if the servers dye their hair."

"You also have a college degree. I thought you were applying for a job that could build a career."

"I have a degree in English. What kind of career is that good for?"

"A lot of things. It's one of those degrees that are all-purpose. You could teach, go into marketing. Even be a writer. Just don't be a novelist. We don't need that kind of scandal in our family."

"Since when has our family cared about its reputation?" she asked, perfectly innocently.

"Yeah, you're right. But remember, Mom's not going to want you to stay here forever. You need a well-paying job to afford rent in a city like this."

"I was planning to live with you, Ma."

That was news to me. I had been hoping to not have an adult child living with me for the rest of my life. Especially not now that I was single.

"I've got work to do," I said.

I went into the cramped sewing room turned magic room

that was my crash pad until I moved into the cottage behind the inn. I sat on the daybed with my laptop and started searching.

Vincent Moulton was not the least bit famous, at least not in the world of data that internet search engines crawled. That real estate agent in Milwaukee was a celebrity compared to the dude in the cemetery. But a few pages into the results, I came across a bit more meat on him.

This Vincent Moulton had achieved his fifteen minutes of fame as Unitarian theologist and a philosopher of Transcendentalism in the early nineteenth century—the philosophy espoused by Ralph Waldo Emerson and Henry David Thoreau.

Why a Unitarian Transcendentalist who died almost two centuries ago would provoke the ire of someone enough to vandalize his grave was beyond me. San Marcos is a city steeped in history. But the vandals must have been steeped in crazy.

To chronicle my efforts, I typed up a short summary of the psychometric findings and the subsequent research. But then, I realized I didn't know how to get it to the Guild. They didn't give me an email address. Hopefully, Laurel would contact me.

When I went downstairs, the wooden horse was gone. The man I had joked with had purchased it.

CHAPTER 11
LEFT IN THE RENTAL CAR

"**B**etter hope your car never ends up here," Detective Samson said.

I surveyed the vast parking lot of cars seized by the city. I saw a surprisingly large proportion of luxury cars, which made me happy, I'm sorry to say.

He led me two rows deep to a Kia. The front plate and a sticker on the windshield flagged it as a rental car. That could prove to be a problem. Liszt's own car would have contained years of memory impressions, but this rental would only have fleeting ones. A police employee was the person who most recently touched the steering wheel, and, before Liszt, would have been the rental car employees and countless customers.

Samson unlocked it, and I got inside. The car still smelled new. I cleared my head, took deep breaths to relax, and grabbed the wheel.

Nothing happened at first. I moved my hands along the wheel's circumference. Finally, I picked up a few stray thoughts about traffic and parking. Complaints about the heat. A Led Zeppelin song popped in my head and then disappeared as if the radio station had changed. Anger about a car cutting the driver off.

To be honest, I didn't know whose thoughts they were.

I handled the gear shifter. And got nothing. No surprise, since you never have your hands on the shifter for long with an automatic transmission.

Was this mission a failure? I glanced around the cabin. If Liszt had spent time in here staking out Danielle, and then me, what would he be doing to kill time?

I tried the radio scan button, thinking he'd be changing channels often. I got a powerful message that a driver hated the radio stations in San Marcos and wished the car had satellite radio. That was all I could pick up.

Samson had wandered away, talking on his phone, so I didn't feel rushed. I tried to clear my thoughts and imagined I was Liszt sitting here for hours. My hands mindlessly strayed to everything within arm's length. I fiddled with the retractable drinking cup holder. My left hand wandered to the side of my seat. It touched the lumbar adjustment lever and—

—*why he wants this stupid coin makes no sense. I've learned everything I could about it, and there's no way Fathead could know where the coin is all the time. It's not a famous piece of artwork. It's just a coin with very little documentation. I almost stole it from the old lady, but after she died, one of her heirs took it immediately. How did Fathead know it ended up with the coin dealer? It makes no sense. It's like he has supernatural powers. Or he's serving someone else with those powers. That's why I think he's some sort of Satan worshipper. Maybe Satan wants the coin. Ha! The devil made him do it! That's a good one! Wait, that cop car is coming around the block again*—

—I still grasped the lumbar control lever, but the memories disappeared for now.

A Satan worshipper? The cemetery vandals mentioned Fathead. Who was he? This was getting strange. But it was clear that Liszt was just an errand boy and didn't know what the true significance of the coin was.

I rubbed my fingers on the adjustment lever, hoping to pick up more memories. Maybe there weren't any. This wouldn't be a lever anyone would touch frequently, unless they had a bad back. Liszt was probably fiddling with it because he was bored. I kept my fingers there for a while, but nothing else came to me.

Samson approached the car.

"Are you done yet?"

"I guess," I said. I stepped out of the car.

"Any psychic surprises?"

"No. I'm certain that someone else hired Liszt, but you already suspected that."

Samson nodded.

"Liszt nicknamed him Fathead. Maybe that will be useful at some point."

"Sure. I'll search mugshots for someone with a fat head."

"You don't have to be so sarcastic," I said.

"Yeah, I do. It's a job requirement."

"Can I see his belongings now?"

He nodded. We returned to his car and drove five blocks to the police station. We rode the elevator to an upper floor and exited into a small lobby. A clerk sat behind a counter working on a computer. Samson handed the young, bearded man a slip of paper and the clerk buzzed us in through a gate. He pointed out an area with a table and three chairs, then disappeared into a storage room with floor-to-ceiling shelves filled with large, gray plastic bins. He returned with a bin and set it on the table.

Inside was a small duffle bag. It appeared to be only half full.

"He travels light," I said.

"His weapon is with ballistics. I'm afraid you're not allowed to handle it."

"That's okay. I have a good idea of what he was thinking while he tried to kill me with it."

I touched the handles of the nylon bag. They had some energy, but it was unfocused. I put the bag on the table.

"Do you mind waiting up front?" I asked Samson. "I can't get in the proper state with someone breathing down my neck."

"No problem." He quickly left. He had better stuff to do than watch me handle stuff.

I zipped open the bag. The zipper gave me a little jolt and feelings of anxiety.

A small amount of clothing was in the bag: shirts, underwear (tighty-whiteys), dress socks. A leather bag with toilet articles. Cellphone charger. Small can of bug spray. Bottle of antacid tablets. And a book.

A book? Liszt didn't seem like the reading type. It was *Looting the Ancient World* by John Rodger. "The theft of antiquities by wealthy collectors," was the subtitle.

That sounded like what Fathead was up to. Was Liszt doing research on his boss? Was Fathead mentioned in the book? I flipped through the pages, but didn't sense any memories. I wouldn't be surprised if Liszt hadn't read it. I knew I couldn't take this particular copy, but I would order the book as soon as possible so I could read it at my leisure and see what it contained.

I touched the clean clothing, which contained nothing. The rolled-up dirty clothes were not something I wanted my hands on. But I forced myself to touch the outer surfaces. No psychic energy that I could feel. Maybe clothing didn't hold memories well.

I opened the leather toilet kit. A shaving razor was tucked into a loop and I touched the handle—

—*man, that was a horrible nightmare. It just went on and on. I look at myself in the mirror and see the bags under my eyes (splash water on my face and apply the shaving cream). I hope my screams weren't audible to the next-door guests. Man, a snake with multiple heads. Isn't that from Greek mythology? But why did my brain cook up a monster like that? (Shave against the grain to get those tricky whiskers on my neck.) I sure hope I don't dream of that snake-thing again. I still can see it—all those jaws snapping at my face. Man, it's so—*

—a hand touched my shoulder.

"Ma'am, are you okay?"

The young man from the front desk looked down at me with concern. "You looked like you were having a seizure."

"I'm fine," I said. "Thank you."

"You were moaning, and your eyes were closed."

"No, really, I'm fine. I must have nodded off."

His expression turned suspicious. He was probably thinking that I was a drug addict.

"I'm finished with this evidence," I said. "Thank you so much."

I got up and quickly walked away.

"Wait," he said. He caught up to me and reached the desk. "I have to buzz you out."

Why did that sound obscene? Probably because celibacy was rotting my brain.

CHAPTER 12
COIN OF THE REALM

S amson was waiting for me by the elevator.

"So, any results?" he asked.

"Nothing useful. I picked up some thoughts he had while shaving in the morning. He was reflecting on a nightmare he'd had about being attacked by a hydra."

"A what?"

"A monster from Greek mythology. A sea serpent with several heads. I wonder if it has any symbolic meaning, but I'm no psychologist."

"Doesn't matter. I would like to find out who this Fathead is, if that was who hired him. Who knows, maybe Fathead also arranged for the prisoner to eat his face."

"So where does the case go from here?" I asked.

"I'm afraid it probably goes nowhere. The suspect in your friend's death was arrested, but killed before we could go to trial. My supervisor considers the case closed, unless I get a new lead that implicates another individual. I probably won't get permission to spend more time on this. So it's up to your . . . gift."

"If I come up with any useful 'psychic silliness' I'll let you know," I said coldly.

"Wait, I didn't say 'silliness.'"

"You thought it."

"What, you can read minds, too?"

I didn't answer, but turned my back and took my leave from the building.

THE COTTAGE BEHIND THE INN FACED THE COURTYARD, WITH its front facade joined to the wall that enclosed the courtyard. It had its own tiny patio at its front door that I stepped across to let myself in with a key I had found in the front desk. The cottage had two bedrooms, one bath, and what would generously be called a kitchenette. It was made for a family to spend a short holiday, not for full-time living. But it would be fine for me. I guessed the structure was built in the early twentieth century, with wall-unit air conditioners added at a later date. It had hardwood floors, a tiny fireplace, and large windows.

Aside from a little mustiness, the place was in good shape and fully furnished. All I needed were linens, towels and my kitchen stuff, and I could move in. I'm sure Mom would be relieved to have one fewer generation living in her house.

I locked up, passed through the main inn, and stepped out the front door. And there, on the narrow sidewalk, sat fellow psychometrist Laurel in her wheelchair.

"Laurel! Have you been out here long?"

"Only a few minutes," she said with a smile. She had such a happy face with chubby cheeks and a button nose. I admired the fact she made no attempt to disguise the streaks of gray in her straight, brown, neck-length hair.

"How did you know I would be here?"

"Word about town was that you bought the inn. And Archibald told me you were here today." Her Southern accent was intoxicating to me after years of hosting northerners at the bed-and-breakfast in Key West.

"I thought he was asleep."

"Gargoyles never truly sleep. Even in stone form, they know what's going on."

"How did he tell you? I didn't think he had a cellphone account."

"He showed up on my stucco wall. Anyway, congratulations on your new business. What are you going to name it?"

I was a bit stumped. "I never even considered changing the name. It's been the Hidalgo Inn for more than a century." The main street in front was Hidalgo Avenue.

"Perhaps you should. You're beginning a new life, and so is the inn."

"Maybe I will," I said. "It seems you already know a lot about me."

"We make it a point to learn about potential clients. That's why we decided to make you an intern."

It felt weird that they knew stuff that I didn't know they knew. But what else should I expect from a supernatural organization?

"Thanks for stopping by," I said. "I don't have a working kitchen yet, so I can't offer you anything. In fact, I haven't moved in yet."

"No worries. I came by to exchange phone numbers with you. It wasn't the proper setting to do so when you met us virtually."

I told her my cell number. She entered it in her phone and texted me with her number.

"I'm adding you to our group text, which is how we usually

communicate. Well, except for Archibald. And Sage, since she's a ghost."

"A guild of supernaturals and paranormals texting each other. It seems so odd to me. But I'm just a regular old girl," I said.

"You're not regular. You're a psychometrist. And a telepath. If we were all telepaths, we wouldn't need to text each other."

"How did you find out I'm a telepath?"

"Gloria, our psychic, sensed it in you."

"Well, I'm not much use as a telepath. People's words sometimes pop into my head, but I've never been able to have an actual conversation, mind to mind, as they say."

"You can work on it. Find someone else with the gift and practice together."

The only person I knew with the "gift," was my mother, as I only just discovered. Even at my age, with more in common with my mother than with my daughter, I couldn't stomach the thought of us getting into each other's minds.

The clip-clop of hooves and the rattle of a carriage rose in volume from around the corner. One of the tourist jitneys was coming.

"How rude of me to keep you out here on the street," I said. "Please come inside."

I admit, I hadn't given much thought to the inn's accessibility, since I'd had so much on my mind. With Laurel at my doorstep, I briefly panicked. The building's original front door, which I was standing outside, required you to step up. Gratefully, I remembered the door on the side street had a ramp. It was where cars pulled up to load or unload luggage.

"Come with me," I said, walking to the corner and taking a right on Cadiz Street. When we reached the short ramp, I grabbed the handles at the back of Laurel's wheelchair and asked her if I could help.

"Heck, no! Don't you see how strong these old arms are?" She cackled with glee and rolled ahead of me.

When I briefly touched the handles, I got a memory fragment from someone other than Laurel. It was about her being seriously injured in a car accident.

I rushed past her to beat her to the door and fumbled with the key chain. I had to try several keys before I found the right one. I needed to label these darned things.

We passed into a foyer that led to the front room to my right, the large sitting room, breakfast room, and kitchen to our left. I realized that this was the proper entrance for guests. The door I'd been using in the front, the original eighteenth-century front door, was no longer appropriate.

"It's just as lovely as I remembered," Laurel said.

"Oh, have you stayed here before?"

"For my honeymoon."

She said nothing more. Her ring finger lacked a wedding ring. The sitting and breakfast rooms both faced the courtyard and were furnished. I led Laurel to the sitting room and sat in a wingback chair that creaked from my weight. All the furniture was antique, but some pieces were looking awfully worn. I would have to give them to Mom to sell.

"Have you had the chance to investigate the cemetery?" Laurel asked.

I studied her eyes for the first time, really. They were a beautiful hazel and twinkled with humor above her little button nose. I liked her. And I enjoyed the sound of her slight Southern drawl.

"Yes, I did. I even wrote up a brief report I can send to you."

I summarized the report, explaining the memories I had read and my research about Reverend Moulton. Laurel nodded her head in agreement.

"Nice job," she said. "You picked up most of the

information."

"Most? There's more?" I had the feeling that Laurel knew more about this than I.

Then, a thought of hers entered my head.

"You had already done a reading of the cemetery," I asked.

"I did. Though I had a hard time touching the upper bars of the fence." She cackled at that.

"So . . . you sent me there to test me?"

Laurel nodded. "And because you might have picked up things I missed. You did find some extra color. 'Fathead,'" she smiled, "that's a good one!"

"What did I miss?"

"Some additional thoughts of Mr. Fathead himself. You got the gist of his intentions, but not his specific mission. Mr. Fathead appears to be a Catholic, and a very conservative one. He has a grudge against Protestants. I think he wishes the Reformation never happened."

"That seems odd in this day and age," I said. "I mean, it's common for religious conservatives to be offended by secular people, but not by other Christian denominations that have been around forever."

"I haven't been able to learn more about his motivations," she said. "But this city was founded when Spanish Catholics were fighting French Protestants."

I knew that well. At the Sangre Inlet, some 500 years ago, a flotilla of French Huguenot soldiers traveled from a settlement to the north to attack San Marcos. They were shipwrecked, and Spanish troops captured them on the beach.

Then, the Spanish massacred all of them.

The Spanish crown wanted to stamp out any attempt by their rivals to colonize in their part of the New World. But the killings were also for religious reasons, at a time when Catholics in France were attacking the Protestant Huguenots, too.

An uneasy feeling came over me when I remembered my vision when holding the coin of men held captive by Spanish soldiers. Was that a memory of the same massacre?

Laurel interrupted my thoughts.

"The Guild is concerned that there has been a concerted effort to erase the legacy of Protestants who have lived in the city. We see vandalism of historical sites all the time, but we're seeing more and more destruction of Protestant history than ever before. Just the other week, some rare volumes of early Lutheran church records were stolen from the university library. I shudder to think they've been destroyed."

"That's so sad," I said.

"We owe it to people who have lived before us to preserve their history and memory. And correct misinformation and disinformation. Think of the American Civil War. Even today, people are arguing for political reasons about why that war was fought, even though there's plenty of contemporaneous documentation that says exactly what the reasons were."

"I'm understanding more about what the Guild does," I said. "Thank you."

"Oh, but there's so much more," she said with a grin.

"Are you working with the police on this war against the Protestant legacy?" I asked.

"No. I don't believe they see it as an organized campaign. They only know of isolated instances of vandalism and theft. Remember, the Guild is a secret. The police don't know about us, though Gloria has worked for them before as a consultant. Some detectives believe psychics can be of value. Most don't."

Yeah, like Detective Samson.

"We know you've been interacting with the police since the death of your friend. Can you share anything about it with me? You asked us to help you, after all."

I began with a terse summary of the night I discovered

Danielle, then my reticence dissolved, my eyes teared up, and I unloaded the entire story on Laurel. There was something about her that made me naturally trust her.

I told her about my first significant experience: touching the bronze angel that had been used to murder Danielle. I told her about the jumble of memories I experienced from the Spanish coin. I recounted in great detail what it was like when Liszt came to Mom's house to kill me and his subsequent arrest. Laurel squinted her eyes in puzzlement when I explained how he had died in the county jail. I concluded with the little bit of information I gleaned from the memories found in his rental car and toilet kit.

"Honey, do you mind if I give my unsolicited opinion?" she asked.

"Go ahead."

"I don't believe another inmate ate the murderer's face. I suspect there's magic at work here. Black magic. That dream he had of the hydra. I think that wasn't just a dream. It was a premonition of his death."

"You think a monster like that killed him?"

"A conjured entity in that form. Yes, I do. We're talking demonic stuff, child. It might be wise to bring the Magic Guild into this."

I didn't say it, but I wasn't sure I wanted to deal with the Magic Guild. Mom had to pay dues to them and keep her magic license current every year, even though she was only a part-time witch. She wasn't fond of their guild and didn't trust their leader, the Arch-Mage Bob.

"Do you happen to have the coin with you?" Laurel asked.

I nodded. "You want to see it?"

"I want to handle it. You've made me very intrigued, especially since someone is willing to kill for it."

I removed it from the bottom of my purse. It was electric in my fingers.

"Are you sure you're ready?" I asked.

"Give it here, honey. I want to teach you something about psychometry. You can learn to control it to some degree. Objects filled with intense energy can pull you right into their worlds and make you feel powerless."

"Tell me about it."

"You need to learn how to avoid that and not get immersed until you're ready. There's a way to stay aloof, and sort of browse through the memories in an object to see if any are worth becoming immersed in. And avoid the ones that appear to be dreadful. On the flip side of that, some objects have only slight traces of memory. Once your mind is trained, you can coax these memories into more vividness."

She held her palm out. "Come on, girl."

I reluctantly placed the coin in her hand. She wrapped her fingers around it and closed her eyes.

"Very, very powerful," she said. "It's amazing that such a tiny coin could be loaded with so many memories. Centuries of memories."

Laurel opened her eyes and locked them onto mine.

"Observe. I will go into a light trance and skim across the surface of the memories. The secret is to maintain a distance between you and the person who left the memory. You do not want to fall into their consciousness. If you feel them pulling you in, you must push back."

It sounded very difficult to me. I watched as Laurel closed her eyes again and tilted her head back. Her breathing slowed.

"My, this coin has passed through many hands," she said in a voice so low that I had to move closer to her to hear. "Most of its owners didn't realize how rare it was. I'm trying to go backward in time with it. I see your friend, but I'm remaining above the memories of her last night. Your friend added the coin to her electronic inventory which collectors could view, before she realized how special it was and removed it from the list. Perhaps, that's how the thief found out about it. Someone named Margaret told your friend about the coin, but I can't sense details of who this Margaret it."

Laurel remained silent for a while.

"Some owners paid a pretty penny for this coin from dealers. Others bought it cheaply from pawn shops or estate sales. Human lives are so brief compared to the existence of a coin like this. They die, their heirs keep it or sell it. It spent years, decades, forgotten in cardboard boxes or fancy chests. But always, eventually, someone finds it, keeps it or passes it along. And so the cycle continues.

"It was even lost at sea once," she continued. "Somehow, years of currents and tides moved it across the sea floor and onto the beach. And can you believe it? It was found by a man with a metal detector.

"It lived in a museum once, here in town. Over a hundred years ago. Until a thief stole it, then pawned it. And thus the cycle continues."

She became silent again. Her breathing remained slow as the minutes ticked by.

But then a moan escaped her lips, and her breathing picked up. She panted, as if running. Sweat beaded upon her forehead.

I was frightened. Should I try to break her trance? Laurel was the experienced one. She might get mad if I intruded.

But she was clearly in distress.

"No, no," she moaned. "I see, I see. No, no."

I touched her arm. Then I shook it.

"Laurel, are you okay?" I shouted.

Her left hand, the one not holding the coin, pushed me away. At least, now her breathing was slowing down. Her head tilted forward until her chin almost touched her chest. She leaned back in her chair as if relaxing.

Then her right arm reached out. Her hand opened and dropped the coin to the floor where it bounced atop the ancient wood.

Finally, her eyes snapped open.

"It almost pulled me in," she said, gasping. "That coin is dangerous. You must be careful with it, Darla. There is death in that coin."

"What do you mean?"

"I broke the connection before I could see exactly what it was, but I knew death was right around the corner. And I don't just mean the memory of death. I believe that coin can kill."

The coin can kill.

"You mean—"

"I mean you can die if you get pulled in too deeply into the death memory. Or memories. Don't do any readings of this coin unless I'm with you. You really shouldn't read it at all anymore."

"I experienced the memory of a soldier held captive by Spanish soldiers," I said. "I'm beginning to believe it was from the massacre at Sangre Inlet in 1565. The one we all had to learn about in school when we were too young to be learning about such things."

"You're lucky you escaped from that memory in time. You could have died along with the French soldier."

"It makes no sense how that could happen. Do you have an explanation?"

"No, except that the memory in the coin is simply too powerful. But probably only someone with our gift would die from it."

Nice to know. So why would you call it a gift if it could kill you?

CHAPTER 13
CAN'T TOUCH THIS

James, the Guild's metal-speaker, was the blacksmith at the reenactment village for the tourists. It was sort of like a permanent Renaissance festival, but devoted to a slightly later time period. I watched James use tongs to pull a metal rod from the fire, place it on an anvil, then beat it with a large hammer.

He was shirtless and wore a heavy leather apron. Arms bulging with muscles, glistening with sweat, he shaped the end of the rod into a curve for some purpose he had explained, but I hadn't heard as I was too intent on the bulging muscles. I wondered if he had a real job on top of this, but realized I didn't care.

After he finished the demonstration, the small crowd applauded, then dispersed from the wooden benches surrounding the smithy. I had to wait for him to finish with two question-askers before I approached.

"You're the new girl. Darla, is it?"

"Yes," I said, not having heard the word "girl" associated with my name for quite some time. "James, right?"

"Yes. What can I do for you?" His bushy brown beard and hair had little flecks of gray. Maybe he wasn't as young as I'd thought.

"I don't know how your metal-speaking works, but can you do it with a coin?"

"A coin? Yes, but they rarely have much to say. They're mass-produced, you know. They spend most of their time in cash registers, vending machines, and coin purses. I can't read the memories of the people who have handled them like you can."

"This is an ancient Spanish coin, from before the founding of San Marcos."

"I could give it a whirl," he said.

"It's overlaid with gold, which I understand is rare for coins."

"It is for coins in general circulation. Do you have it with you?"

"In my purse. Can you look at it somewhere private?"

"Come with me." He went into an adjacent toolshed that was also set up to look like the blacksmith's sleeping quarters. I hoped this wasn't where he actually slept.

"Have a seat." He gestured to a small table and two chairs. The rest of the space held tools and a cooler. No bed, I was relieved to see. "Let me see what you've got."

I sat down and rummaged through my purse until I found the coin. This wasn't the best way to store the precious item, but thieves would probably give up once they saw how much junk was in the bag.

He held the coin by its edge and studied both sides.

"Hm, early sixteenth century. Minted in the New World, probably Mexico. The gold covering looks like it was added later. Let's see what she can tell me."

He held the coin between his forefingers and thumbs, rubbing it with his thumbs in a circular motion. It was almost as if he was trying to clean it. He did this to both sides, then held it in his palms with his hands pressed together as if in prayer.

He closed his eyes and appeared to go into a trance like Laurel had. I hoped he wouldn't find anything scary like she did. After some time, he opened his eyes and placed the coin on the table.

"I was wrong. The coin was minted in Spain, not the New World. But the silver was from Mexico. As was the gold. The coin came back to the New World as part of a shipment of monies to pay the occupying troops. But the gold was looted from an Aztec temple and added to the coin by a skilled metalsmith in Mexico. The gold has a troubled history."

"What do you mean?"

"As I said, it was from a sacramental object. I believe, a bowl meant for collecting the blood of children sacrificed to the gods. There is a lot of negative energy in this gold. The bowl was stolen and melted down, poured into a mold atop the silver of the coin."

"Why was the coin altered like that?"

He looked at me and raised a bushy eyebrow. "Same reason people make jewelry. To make it prettier or more symbolic. More valuable. To make it a keepsake instead of a mere coin to exchange for goods and services."

"Why do the designs on the gold look like they were based on the indigenous culture if a Spaniard added them?"

"I didn't say it was a Spaniard. I said it was a skilled metalsmith."

"Do you think there was religious meaning behind the coin's alteration?"

"I think you answered your own question."

"I have another," I said. "Do you think the coin is evil?"

He gave me an odd look. "Evil? It's not enchanted, if that's what you mean."

"Don't you think the gold was, well, evil, because of what the bowl was used for?"

"Not in the Aztecs' perspective. Maybe in the mind of whoever had the work done. But there's a good chance he or she didn't know where the gold had come from. All I can say is that the coin itself has not been used for anything evil. I do sense it may have changed hands as the result of violence. Money has a way of being associated with violence, doesn't it?" he said with an ironic laugh.

"I think it may have been in the possession of a Huguenot soldier who died in the massacre at Sangre Inlet. How would he have a Spanish coin?"

"The early French settlements in the Southeast, before the Spanish wiped them out, were active in piracy against the Spanish treasure fleets. The fleets rode the Gulf Stream north, up the coast of Florida from the Caribbean and Central America, before turning east to cross the Atlantic to Spain."

"If the French soldier had this coin before he was executed, the Spanish probably took it from him afterwards," I said.

"No doubt."

"Well, thank you, James, for your help."

"No problem at all. Can I ask you a question?"

"Sure."

"Where did you get the coin?"

"From my friend. A rare coin dealer who was murdered by someone searching for this coin."

"Wow." His face softened. "I'm sorry to hear that. My condolences."

"Thank you. The coin is full of memories, including those of the soldier killed in the massacre. Laurel said it's dangerous. And that the memories could kill a psychometrist."

"I've never heard of such a thing."

"Yeah, I learned to never touch a live wire or hot stove. Who knew a coin could be dangerous, too?"

After I took my leave, I pondered, again, why the coin was so desired by whoever had hired Liszt. What was so special about the coin other than its deadliness? And the deadliness was only for psychometrists. The coin was undoubtably rare, with its overlay of gold, but rare enough to kill for?

And how did the collector even know about it before it appeared on the electronic inventory?

I needed to find out what happened after the French soldier died. I decided to read the coin again, going backward in time, but stopping safely before reaching the point when the soldier was killed.

Lauren had told me that I shouldn't read the coin without her with me. But, she wouldn't approve of what I wanted to do. She would tell me not to do it. I was certain that if I was careful, I could jump in, get a brief glimpse of what I was looking for, then jump right out.

Was I being foolish? Probably. That wasn't going to stop me.

I went to Mom's house. Sophie was manning the counter, which she did when she wasn't working at the restaurant. It was her way of paying rent. I went upstairs to the second floor, where Mom was setting out some silverware for sale. I would think she should display the silverware downstairs in the former dining room, but Mom had her own system. It was called chaos.

"Mom, I'm going up to the sewing room—"

"Magic room."

"Yes. How could I forget? I'm going to do a little psychometric experiment. If you don't hear from me in, say, half an hour, could you check on me?"

"Why?" she asked with alarm.

"In case I have trouble coming out of a trance."

She nodded, but stared at me with suspicion.

Up in the magic room, I sat on the daybed and retrieved the coin from my purse. It hummed particularly strongly today.

Boy, I hope I'm not taking too much of a risk. Famous last words.

I felt myself plunging into the memory of a pawn-shop owner examining the coin, presented to him by a young woman who looked strung out on drugs. But I stopped myself. I pushed back. Like Laurel had instructed, I remained above the memory. And then I moved on.

I didn't have the skill yet to rewind back through the years in an orderly fashion. The memories skipped around a lot among different people from different time periods. But I was gradually going back in time.

The coin is handed down from a father to daughter, kept in a small wooden box with a parchment.

Years pass sitting idle in a chest stored in a stone room.

The coin is placed in the polished box with the piece of parchment.

A retired soldier is writing on the parchment on a table lit by a single candle.

Death was near. Not involving the man scratching the parchment with his quill, but someone he knew. He has witnessed this death.

I sank into the memories of the man writing in tiny script upon the paper, the coin in his left hand. The coin was harmless to him. But he wrote of—

—*Carlos had taken the coin from the Huguenot after killing him. Looting bodies was disgusting to me, but all our men did it. Perhaps it was fair compensation for the horrible butchery we were forced to perform. Carlos had told me when the heretic died, he was clutching the coin in his hand like we would hold the rosary. For comfort. To be closer to God. This is what Carlos said to me, just after his act of killing. He said, "The Frenchman saw the face of God as he died." I told him you cannot take the delirious words of a dying man so literally. But Carlos insisted the words were true. He said he saw the man's face light up with pure ecstasy like he'd never before seen in a dying man's face. He said the Frenchman seemed to glow with the Holy Spirit. Carlos was convinced that the man had, in fact, been graced with the sight of God's face.*

A fortnight hence, we were back in San Marcos. Carlos and I were in a tavern, deep in our cups, and he said to me he had a gift. Sometimes, he could touch objects and see the lives of those who had owned them. I said this was nonsense, but he only smiled. He said, "I shall hold the coin of the Huguenot and see if I can see his life. I want to read his thoughts when he died. Maybe I, too, can see the face of God in a vision passed to me from the Frenchman through the coin."

"You are spouting drunken nonsense," I said. We both were weary, as were all the men, after our engagements with the French and all the slaughter we had wrought. We were tired to the bone, to our very souls. It was only natural Carlos should have such thoughts, as if he was a mad saint. But he proceeded to drain his cup of wine. The coin was in a leather pouch he had found, probably on another executed prisoner. He removed the coin, and I saw it had a special design and would be worth much. But it didn't seem magical to me.

Carlos held the coin in both hands and soon appeared to fall asleep. Moments later, he moaned as if in pain. He mumbled incomprehensible words. Then he raised his head, eyes still closed, and said, "I am dying, I am dying, and I see the face of the Lord, bright with the light of heaven behind him. The Father, the Son, and the Holy Spirit are as one, smiling at me. And there is more: It is glorious, glorious. My God, it is miraculous. It is more than I can describe. It is glorious!" And then he dropped to the table.

Carlos was stone-dead. I saw it right before my eyes, and it was whatever he saw in the coin that killed him, I am certain. I have touched the coin, and to me it was nothing but silver covered with gold. I even showed it to our priest, who saw nothing in it. Yet, Carlos saw a secret in it that killed him. Keep this coin in safekeeping, for it is rare and magical.

But beware of arousing the magic that killed Carlos. I attest to the truth of what I—

—was being roughly shaken by Mom as I lay sprawled upon the daybed.

"Let go of that coin," she said, wrenching my hand open, so the coin dropped to the quilt.

"What happened," I asked, knowing perfectly well the answer.

"You were moaning, having a terrible nightmare. Your practice session with the coin was a bad idea."

"Yeah, I guess it was."

"I thought you said you met another psychometrist from the Memory Guild who was helping you. Why were you doing this alone?"

Even crazy mothers like mine showed a lot of common sense when it came to their children.

"You're absolutely right, Mom. I should have known better."

"Put that coin away and do something useful. There's a chicken in the fridge. Please prepare it for supper."

"Thanks for looking out for me," I said. And I meant it.

When she left the room, I reflected on what I had learned. The coin allegedly held the memory of a man who had seen the face of God. It seemed like an appealing concept, but very far-fetched.

The scary thing was Carlos had died after reading this memory. He had apparently had the ability of psychometry and died because of it. The death that Laurel had sensed in the coin was real.

The rational part of my brain struggled to accept these ideas. But if the coin actually held the memory of a man who had seen the face of God when he died, you could say the coin itself held the image of God's true visage.

The coin would be extremely valuable to a very religious

person who believed this. Maybe even enough to kill in order to get the coin.

I needed to report my findings to Laurel. She would be angry with me, but I would have to take my punishment.

The question remained: How did the person who sought the coin learn about its special power?

I needed to find this Margaret, whose name both Laurel and I had heard in our reading of the coin. She was a contemporary person, someone Danielle knew. I hoped she could help me.

ACCORDING TO OUR READINGS, IT WAS MARGARET WHO HAD discovered how rare the coin was and told Danielle. But Danielle had never mentioned the name to me. So I had to search blindly. I assumed Margaret was involved with antiquities or historical research of some kind. My first act was to search the online directory of the faculty at the local college. I found one Margaret, but she was a biochemist. It wasn't likely to be her.

Next, I went to one of the city's historical museums. San Marcos was said to be the oldest continuously inhabited city in the U.S. There were a lot of museums. Some were really just tourist traps, like the Old Jail, but others were more legitimate. One of them chronicled the archeological digs that were ongoing in the city. It was a smaller facility with exhibits showing some of the finds from the digs, ranging from the Native American Timucuan people to the present day.

A docent, an elderly man with a cane, asked me if I wanted a tour.

"Actually," I said, "I was wondering if anyone by the name of Margaret works here."

"Oh, our assistant director is Margaret Peabody, is that who you mean?"

"Perhaps. All I know is her first name. Is she here today? My name is Darla Chesswick."

The docent looked at me like I was a nut, but left the room. Not long afterwards, a middle-aged woman with her hair in a buzz cut approached me.

"I'm Margaret Peabody."

"Hi! I'm Darla. Thanks for speaking to me. I'm doing some research, and someone gave me the name Margaret. I'm hoping it's you."

"Who gave you my name?"

"You wouldn't know her. She doesn't know you. Actually, it's a really long, strange story, as so many things in life are. . ."

Margaret showed signs of losing patience.

"I'm looking for an artifact from the early Colonial era and hoped you might know something about it. It's a carved wooden box that contained a parchment with information about a Spanish coin that presumably had been in the box as well, but has gone its own way since. A very rare coin."

"A letter about a coin?" Her eyes narrowed.

"Yes." I knew I sounded crazy. The docent should have told her I was a nut.

"We did have such an item," she said. "It was stolen from the museum over a year ago. I always thought it odd, because we have antique coins here that could sell for good money, but this was a box with nothing but a letter in it."

"I believe there's a person who is searching for the coin. I think he stole the box and letter. Either to learn more about the coin. Or it's through the letter that he discovered the coin exists. Did your exhibit have a transcript of the letter?"

"Just a brief summary. It would have been controversial if we transcribed the entire letter. There's a reference in it to seeing the face of God. The exhibit was a portrayal of life back in the early years of the city. We assumed the box was a gift meant to be sent back to relatives in Spain."

"I think it was to prevent the wrong people from touching the coin. And dying like the soldier the letter writer describes."

"Wait a moment, you've seen the letter!" Margaret said, almost clutching my arm but stopping herself. "Where is it? Do you have it?"

I didn't know how to lie my way out of this completely.

"You could say I'm a psychic of sorts. I had a vision of the soldier who wrote the letter."

Margaret gave me a skeptical look. "What did you say your name was?"

"Darla Chesswick. And no, I don't know where the letter is. If you're planning on calling the police, ask for Detective Samson. He'll vouch for me. My friend, a coin dealer, was murdered by someone looking for the coin that used to be in the box. I'm trying to find out how they learned about the coin. It sounds like the stolen letter tipped them off."

I turned away from her and her astonished expression.

"Thank you for your time," I said as I left the room.

CHAPTER 14
THE ATTIC

The cottage behind the inn had basic furnishings. I could have moved in with only a few purchases of linens and such. But I remained in Mom's magic room, sleeping on the uncomfortable day bed, surrounded by the magic supplies that gave me nightmares. After my latest unsettling experience with the coin, I felt better staying in a home with people around.

But now, enough of that. The togetherness grew old quickly. The very day the movers showed up with my stuff from Key West, I was out of there.

My "stuff" included hardly any furniture. I sold the bed-and-breakfast in Key West the same way I bought the inn here: contents included. I did ship my mattress and box spring, though, since I'm very particular about that. Most of what lay piled up in the inn's foyer were personal belongings. I'm not a pack rat like Mom, but I still had dozens of boxes of books, mementoes and select kitchen items I couldn't do without, as well as several prints and canvases by local artists from both Key West and San Marcos.

And Cory's art photographs. I still hung onto them for some reason.

In short, I had too much junk to fit in the cottage. I'd have to keep much of it here in the main building. I sure wish it had an attic that didn't keep disappearing.

I mention this because it happened again today. I was on the third floor, walking down the main hallway, when I passed an extra door in between two guest rooms.

Wait, the linen closet was across the hall. Was this an extra closet I had overlooked? I tried the handle, but it was locked, which was odd since none of the closets on this floor had locks. Fortunately, I had the keyring with me and tried a half dozen keys, but none worked.

Without thinking, I tried the handle again. Oh, it wasn't locked after all.

When I opened the door, I was shocked to find stairs rising up into darkness. They were of raw wood, darkened with time, with unfinished walls of shiplap and studs on each side. They turned ninety degrees to the left at the top, and I could see nothing else. There was no light switch at the bottom of the steps and no lightbulb anywhere along the ceiling.

I couldn't believe this door was here. Before, the presence of the attic was given away by the trapdoor in the ceiling that had disappeared. This seemed much more substantial than a trapdoor with a folding ladder. This seemed permanent, even though I hadn't noticed it before.

I ran downstairs to get a flashlight.

When I returned, I half expected the door to have disappeared, but it was still there. I turned on the flashlight, aimed the beam on the steps and climbed slowly, feeling the risers sag slightly with each step, causing unnerving creaks.

As I climbed, a headache hit me out of nowhere. A strong feeling of anxiousness and dread came over me. I didn't think this was the doing of my imagination. Soon, the bones of my legs and arms ached. I felt nauseous. It was as if I were going into a nuclear reactor.

Some primitive part of my brain recoiled at whatever unseen thing was ahead of me. It was just pure, raw fear. Of what, I didn't know. I tried to convince myself to ignore my imagination, but I was quickly losing my determination to continue climbing.

I was nearing the point where the stairs turned left. Where the wall blocked my view of the top of the stairs, the air was shimmering. It wasn't floating dust motes; there was a blurry film obscuring my vision. It was like looking through a waterfall at what was behind it.

My dizziness grew stronger and my legs felt weak. My hands trembled.

It was time to retreat. I slowly climbed down the stairs, but I didn't turn around. I went backwards, not wanting to turn my back on whatever was up there.

When I reached the bottom, I backed into the well-lit hallway and instantly felt better. I closed the door. I tried the handle, and it was locked, now.

Maybe I was coming down with the flu or something. Exploring the attic would have to wait for another time.

I went back downstairs and spent the rest of the day sorting through my newly arrived belongings. Boxes of kitchen stuff went into the cottage, followed by linens and towels. I switched the mattress on the bed with my own and made it with my sheets. Then I put my personal items in the bathroom and dragged the wardrobe box into the main bedroom, transferring my clothes into the dresser and closet. I made a note to buy a jacket and a few sweaters. Unlike Key West, San Marcos would be chilly on winter nights and mornings.

I carried one box of books to the cottage, plus two paintings and boxes of personal items and financial records. The rest of the books and other junk would remain in the main building until I figured out where to put it.

I tossed out the cheap coffee maker in the cottage and set up my expensive one that I quickly set to work brewing a pot. I refused to use those pod things for my coffee. An old-fashioned drip machine was just fine for me.

Sipping a fresh cup, I rummaged through one of the boxes, setting out knickknacks to make the cottage feel more like home. A sea trout carved from driftwood went on the coffee table. I put a basket of rare seashells that I had collected over the years on an end table.

Then I came upon a mahogany box. Inside was a magnifying glass my second husband Cory used to read fine print. His eyeglasses were in there, too. He didn't wear them all the time, mostly when reading or driving.

It had always felt strikingly odd that he had left them on a table in our living room the night he disappeared nearly a year ago. I'd heard of husbands slipping out of the house, claiming they were going to the store, only to never return, leaving their family and all their possessions behind.

But his eyeglasses? Why would he leave those behind? He left all his expensive camera gear, too.

When Cory left, he didn't tell me he was going to the store. He just left. We were hanging out in the living room. Cory had turned off the TV, and we were reading books before it was time to go to bed. I got up, went into the bathroom attached to the master bedroom. When I came out, he wasn't in the room. I figured he was in the other bathroom. After a while, I checked. He wasn't there. He wasn't anywhere in our apartment. I searched the grounds of the bed-and-breakfast and never found him.

He was gone.

When I had been in the bathroom, there was no sound of

the front door opening and closing. He had slipped out like a ninja.

He didn't write a note. I left so many messages on his cellphone that his voicemail box became full. He didn't mail me a letter. I never heard from him again.

The strangest thing about it was the fact that our marriage was great. There had been no recent arguments or tension. We communicated freely. Things were great in bed.

We first met in a bookstore where he was doing a signing for his second book of nature photographs. I haunted bookstores regularly, back in the days when they were abundant. I had been an English major and planned to become a professor, but then Buddy wanted to get married. I ended up as an office worker for an insurance company.

Watching Cory sign his books that evening made him a celebrity in my eyes. I couldn't really afford it, but I bought the expensive coffee-table book so he could sign it. He asked me to have coffee afterwards, and we soon became friends. After I divorced Buddy, I looked up Cory and our friendship resumed. And soon became much more.

My occasional telepathy didn't bother Cory. He joked that it kept him honest. In fact, he was fascinated by my gift. It turned out he had an interest in the paranormal and supernatural. He believed fervently in ghosts and wanted to photograph one someday.

The truth was, there wasn't much money in being a nature photographer, so Cory also taught at the local college. On vacation in Key West a few years into our marriage, we came across a bed-and-breakfast that was for sale. We abandoned all caution and made an offer. It turned out that we both enjoyed being innkeepers. Until he left, of course.

Cory was tall and thin, with straight brown hair parted in the middle that he always allowed to grow a little too long. He had slate-gray eyes and shaved every day. He never smoked, never drank to excess, and was warm and loving. In fact, he treated Sophie like she was his own child. I would have said he was almost perfect, but, of course, there was his great betrayal. And I had tried to be as perfect a wife as I could.

There was no reason he should have wanted to leave. He just did.

I figured he had grown tired of me. Or was having a male midlife crisis and wanted to start his life over somewhere else. And, after my first, disastrous marriage, I guess I wasn't so surprised my second wouldn't end well either. But it shouldn't have ended. We were doing great.

Let me tell you, ghosting your spouse is not the proper way to end a relationship. Don't make your spouse spend the rest of his or her years wondering what happened to you.

Thinking about the night he disappeared, I remembered the nausea that had flooded my stomach when I entered the living room to find he wasn't there. At that moment, I had figured he was in the other room. I hadn't yet realized he was gone. But the anxious nausea had filled me as if some part of my brain knew what had really happened.

Darla Chesswick had failed at two marriages. And here I was, in middle-age, the Change beginning in my body. Was it even worthwhile to try at love again?

I stepped out into the courtyard to clear my head and noticed the gate to the street was partly open. When I went to close it, Esmerelda was standing there.

"Hello, Darla," she said with an overly perky smile. "Sorry to startle you. I was walking down the street and noticed your gate was open. I just took a little peek inside. I'm just so nosy!"

"Would you like me to show you around?" I asked. I didn't want to, but felt like I had no choice. There was no reason to be unfriendly to her, and I wanted to prove that I had absolutely no resentment that she was with bonehead Buddy.

"Why, that would be so kind of you. Just a quick look around would be fine. I'm an event planner and your inn would be a great place for a smaller event."

That was true. I couldn't let any potential business slip away. So I gave her a look inside the cottage. I told her I was living there now, but should rooms ever be in great demand I would consider moving out so I could offer it to guests. I showed her the breakfast room, which was large enough to hold a luncheon or intimate wedding reception. The living room would be perfect for the ceremony. She marveled at the Medieval fireplace in the front room, having no idea that one of the gargoyles was supernatural. I took her quickly through the second floor, spending a little more time in what I suddenly deemed to be the "honeymoon" suite, which had a hot tub and a balcony over-looking the courtyard. We took a quick tour of the third floor, though I avoided showing her the haunted room. And then, as we were about to make our way downstairs, I noticed something.

The door to the attic was missing. No sign at all of it. At this point, it didn't surprise me.

"Anything wrong?" Esmerelda asked. She must have seen a shocked expression on my face.

"Nothing at all. I just remembered something I'd forgotten to do."

"Well, I'll get out of your hair," she said.

When we reached the foyer, she thanked me for the tour and apologized again for peeking into the courtyard.

"No problem at all," I said. "Once I get the inn up and running, I'd love for you to see it again, when it's looking more presentable."

"That would be lovely. And Darla, I wanted to say that I hope we can be friends. Buddy doesn't have any grudge against you and only says nice things. And I look forward to meeting Sophie soon."

"Grudge" was a reference to the fact that I had thrown Buddy out. Doing so wasn't unreasonable after he had blown all our savings, wrecked our car, been bailed out of jail twice, and then cheated on me with a bartender.

I smiled. "Buddy has a heart of gold."

I wanted to gag after saying that.

We said goodbye, and I led her out the proper way, through the main entrance. After she disappeared down the street, I went around to close and lock the gate.

The gate hung from hinges attached to a wooded beam affixed to the edge of the opening in the stone wall. The wall was old, maybe even older than the house, and was made with large blocks of limestone created naturally over millennia by tiny coquina shells. I had noticed before that a small piece of stone a couple of inches wide at the wall's edge had cracked loose. It had remained resting in its niche in the wall, and now it was missing. I couldn't find it anywhere on the ground.

I needed to find a way to patch the gap in a manner that naturally blended with the stone. I had no clue how to do so. This was just one of the million little things that needed to be fixed or improved that were popping up on my to-do list.

Why did I have to buy an old building? Because I always had to make things unnecessarily difficult for myself, that's why.

Just as I was closing the gate, a loud *meow* came from the sidewalk. It sounded like "*no*."

I opened the gate slightly, and a black cat slipped into the courtyard. It looked up at me expectantly.

"Hello there," I said. "Are you welcoming me to the neighborhood?"

The cat rubbed itself against my lower leg.

"You're in luck. I have some tuna in my box of staples. Wait right here while I get it."

I entered the cottage and rummaged through the box on the small island counter. I found a small snack-sized can and opened the pop-top lid. Before I dumped it on a small plate, something soft rubbed against my leg.

The black cat looked up at me. He or she seemed to smile.

"How did you get in here? I thought I closed the door."

The cat said, *"no"* again. Sure enough, the door was slightly open.

I emptied the can on the plate and placed it on the floor where the cat devoured it. He looked up at me again.

"That's all I've got," I said. "I'll buy some cat food later if you're still around."

He rubbed my leg again and strolled over to a wicker chair in the corner. He jumped into the chair, curled up on the cushion, and closed his eyes.

"I didn't invite you to stay," I said. "You probably have fleas."

Life was tough for stray cats. As soon as I had time, I would bring him to the vet to check him out and see if he had a chip. I know it was sexist to call it a "he," but I hadn't given him an intimate examination yet, and that was the pronoun that people used when talking about a critter of unknown gender.

For now, he could hang out. It would be nice to have someone to keep me company here besides a vampire, a gargoyle, and at least one ghost. Even if my new friend always told me *"no."*

CHAPTER 15
FOWL BOWELS

The next day began with poop.

Bird poop.

The inn was only two blocks from the bay, so I often was visited by great blue herons and white egrets hunting for lizards in my courtyard or stalking the cobblestone street feeding on insects. Seagulls would often fly by, but they never stuck around.

Until today.

I had a long list of things to buy at the home improvement store, but stopped in my tracks as soon as I walked down the side street and saw my car parked halfway down.

It was white. And that was a problem, because my car was actually black. I walked up to it, trying to convince myself that it wasn't my car, that I had forgotten where I'd actually parked.

But it *was* my car. Covered from hood to trunk in white bird poop.

I'd never seen anything like this before. Crows had a dislike of my car, and if I was ever foolish enough to park beneath a tree, the crows would decorate my car with splashes and splotches of poop on the roof and running down the windows, like abstract artists flinging white paint on a canvas. My car had suffered cruel attacks before, but nothing like this. There was barely any black paint or clean glass visible. The poor little Ford lay under a giant white tarp made of bird poop. The street and sidewalk next to my car hadn't been spared either.

I hadn't parked near a tree, so I blamed seagulls. They pooped as prolifically as crows, but only as they flew by overhead, not in a deliberate fashion while perched on tree branches like the crows. So this carpet bombing of my car made no sense.

Maybe vandals had done it. Maybe this was paint or some other substance.

I peered closely at my white windshield. It wasn't pure white. There were flecks of blacks and browns in it. Like bird poop.

Any doubts left my mind when a hot splat landed on my head. And then another one.

I looked up and saw the seagulls circling overhead. A splash landed on my right cheek. I swore, unlocked my car, and dove inside, getting hit in the neck before I reached safety.

My shock soon turned into anger as I cleaned myself with tissues as best I could. I was determined to carry on with my errand, even if my car attracted stares along the way and in the store's parking lot. I started the engine and turned on the windshield wipers, pulling on the rod to spray wiper fluid.

The wipers merely smeared the white goo, which had nearly dried like paint. But I wasn't giving up.

However, every time I managed to see a little bit through the windshield, bird poop rained down upon it, making me blind again.

I couldn't believe the intentionality of this attack. It wasn't just coincidental—they seemed truly to be out to get my car.

It sank in that I wasn't going anywhere if I couldn't clean my windshield enough to see through it. I had to go back to the inn and get some rags and window cleaner.

Just as I opened the door, two bird bombs hit my arm. I slammed the door shut. What the heck was I supposed to do? Call the police and say I was being assaulted by seagulls? Call a towing service to take me to a carwash?

Of course, Alfred Hitchcock's *The Birds* came to mind. But that was just a movie. This was real life, gone to poop.

I decided to make my escape. I jumped out of the car and ran towards the inn. A vast flock of seagulls followed, raining their excrement upon me. Individual birds made dive-bombing runs at close range.

My head collided with one of them, its talons briefly becoming entangled in my hair. I suppressed the urge to scream.

I reached the main entrance of the inn and jumped under the awning that covered the walkway, but as I neared the door, two great blue herons appeared, blocking my way. They squawked angrily at me. This species was tall. I wasn't much taller. They strode on their long, spindly legs toward me, beaks snapping.

I ran away. I headed around the corner to the original front door, getting drenched by bird poo the entire way. Now it wasn't just seagulls above me; terns and ibis were emptying their bowels on me, too. My crow enemies were there as well.

But a squad of large white egrets guarded the door, angrily hissing. Their beaks snapped as they marched toward me.

I ran past the door, along the length of the inn to the narrow alley. I turned left and ran past the garbage bin, toward the east gate in the wall of my courtyard. I pulled my keyring from my purse and struggled to find the right key as the poop rained down on me.

What if a neighbor saw me? Would they think I was a white wraith?

I found the right key and entered the courtyard. I should have known.

Pigeons. The entire ground of my courtyard was wall-to-wall

pigeons. As I tried to push through them, they rose like a giant gray blanket. The flapping of thousands of wings buffeting me with wind.

And then the poop storm went from bad to biblical proportions. So much bird poop drenched me, I couldn't see as I headed for the patio doors.

The image of planes and helicopters dropping water on wildfires came to mind. Here, the birds were trying to extinguish me.

Trying desperately not to get any poop in my mouth or eyes, I plodded with determination toward the door. By now, I was certain that magic was at work here. Some witch or wizard was doing this to me. Probably warning me to stop investigating Danielle's death.

Maybe because their bowels were finally empty, or because they were ordered to, the birds stopped pooping.

Instead, they began to attack.

A sharp beak struck the top of my head, followed by another. I flailed my arms above me, hitting birds but also getting pecked hard. Red blood appeared through the white that coated me.

This was truly turning out Hitchcock-like.

Great blue herons stood in front of the patio door. Across the courtyard, egrets guarded the doors to my cottage. Once the birds started attacking *en masse*, I would be doomed.

I moved to a courtyard wall, so at least my back would be protected. I tripped on something. It was a shovel I had left there while planting the other day. I grabbed it. The shovel was my only hope.

There I stood, my back against the wall of coquina stone, making my last stand. I swung the shovel at an attacking seagull and slapped it. The shovel was awkward to use like a bat, but I kept swinging, whacking seagulls and crows. The other birds kept their distance, circling overhead.

A bird landed on my head, grasping my hair. I shook my head frantically, and the bird dropped to the ground.

I kept swinging, but the birds got the message. They kept out of reach. Soon the tops of the walls and the roofs of the inn and cottage were packed solidly with perching birds.

I walked toward my cottage, brandishing the shovel. And suddenly, as if they all heard the same command, the mass of birds rose into the sky and flew away. My courtyard and roofs were covered with bird poop and resembled a snowy landscape. The sky was sunny with no chance of rain to wash away the "snow."

And in case you're wondering, my shovel didn't kill any birds. When I thought I was fighting for my life, I would have had no qualms about taking a bunch of them out. But now, I was glad they all survived. It wasn't their fault they were under some evil influence.

My new friend, the black cat, trotted into the courtyard.

"Where the heck were you when I needed you? I thought cats love to attack birds."

No, he said.

"Right. Only when you're not outnumbered thousands to one."

It was time for a long shower. And then a consultation with a witch.

My mother finally stopped laughing when I got to the part about being pecked and bleeding. Good for her, because I was about to lose my temper with her big time.

"So what do you think?" I asked. We were sitting in her kitchen. I tried to relax with some chamomile tea. It was difficult ignoring the voices of customers in the front of the house joking about the car caked with bird crap that was parked outside. No, I hadn't stopped at a carwash yet.

"It sounds like a hostile magic attack," Mom said. "Have you angered any witches?"

"Not that I know of, assuming I didn't anger you."

"Not enough for a spell like that."

"It could be related to the coin," I said. "I guess the person seeking it knows about me. But I don't know what this magic attack was supposed to accomplish other than scaring me to death. And humiliating me, for some reason. That was part of it, too."

"Scaring you enough to give up the coin?"

"Maybe. Except now, I'm even more anxious to find out who's behind this."

"You should go to the Magic Guild. They can help you figure out what you've been hexed with. And, in my view, enchanting the birds to attack you is against the Guild's laws."

"I thought you didn't want anything to do with the Guild." I said.

"Yes, I dislike all their bureaucratic crap, and I can't stand Arch-Mage Bob. But, since I'm forced to pay dues every year, I may as well get my money's worth."

"I don't know if I want a bunch of strangers in my business. I don't want them to find out that I have the coin and leak that information."

"Good point." Mom sipped her tea reflectively. "There's always your cousin, Missy."

Missy was a witch who lived in South Florida. I had never even known about her for most of my life because of bad blood between Mom and her sister, Missy's mother, who had given her up for adoption. It's a long story.

"I don't know if I should ask Missy for another favor. She helped me so much with Sophie."

Sophie had gotten herself into a dangerous situation with an addiction-recovery company in Missy's town. That's another long story.

"You wouldn't tell me exactly what Missy did," Mom said.

Yep. I didn't want Mom to know how dangerous the whole thing had been.

"Missy's magic helped us find Sophie and get her out of that horrible sober home."

"If you don't think Missy can help you more than the witches and wizards of the Guild. . ."

"Actually, I do. Missy's a powerful spell-caster." That's as much as I would reveal.

"Then call her and see what she says."

I nodded my agreement and sipped my tea. Mom slipped into the front rooms to mind the store. Distant thunder brought hope to my heart that a good rain was coming and would rinse off my car and courtyard.

"MISSY, IT'S DARLA," I SAID INTO MY PHONE.

"Darla! How are you? How's Sophie?"

"We're fine," I said. "I hate to call you with an agenda, but I need your advice on the topic of magic."

"How can I help you?"

"I was the victim of a magic attack today."

"Oh, my," she said.

I described my misadventures with the bird turds. I then mentioned vaguely that I may have crossed someone very powerful.

"Oh, my," she said. "Can I come up and give you a hand?"

"That would be too kind of you. I feel so defenseless."

"Isn't your mother a witch?"

"Witchcraft is just a hobby for her. And, let me be honest with you. My friend was murdered, and I have in my possession what the murderer was seeking. I don't want my mother involved in any of this."

"But your cousin is a different story?"

"My cousin is a powerful witch who can kick butt," I replied. "To be fair, I should fill you in on everything that's been going on."

I told her about the murder, about Liszt, about his attack on me. I gave a summary of my investigation into the cemetery vandalism, because I believed the same culprits were involved in both.

Finally, I told her everything I knew about the Spanish coin, and all the memories I had read in it.

"Oh, my," she said. "You're up to your eyeballs in quite a mystery."

"And then, there's the magic being used against me. Now you see why I need your help so badly."

"Let me try to clear my schedule, and I'll drive up there as soon as I can."

CHAPTER 16

MY COUSIN MISSY

T he very next day, a loud rattling and sputtering came from Cadiz Street outside the courtyard. A cloud of gasoline exhaust drifted overhead. What pitiful excuse of a motor vehicle was that?

It was Missy's Toyota sedan, which, last time I saw it, had nearly a half a million miles on its odometer. The poor, undying monster crouched by the inn's entrance, rattling as if it had a palsy. When she turned off the engine, the car shook as if dying for good.

I went around to the driver's side as Missy stiffly exited. She was in her midlife like me, and no one our age does well with a four-hour drive.

We hugged and cheek-kissed.

"Thanks for getting up here so quickly," I said.

"I was worried about you. If you're a victim of black magic, it could be serious."

"I feel better with you here. So how was the drive?"

"Painful for both of us," Missy said. "My back is killing me, and poor Bessie here needed two quarts of oil along the way."

"Is it time to put Bessie down?"

"Never," Missy said. Then, she smiled. "Never underestimate the durability of Japanese engineering. And a bit of magic. I give her a different spell every five thousand miles."

"Thanks for coming up. I still owe you too much for helping me out with Sophie," I said, and I meant it.

"That's what cousins are for."

There wasn't much family resemblance between us. Missy was rather tall, at least compared to me, and had straight brown hair with bangs, not the jet-black hair of the Chesswick clan. Our mothers were sisters and, based on an old photo, her mother looked more like a Chesswick with a dimpled chin and freckles. Missy looked more French than Irish.

"Not knowing how long I'll need to stay, I brought the fur babies," Missy said.

She opened the rear door and pulled out two pet carriers. The cats inside protested meekly.

"They can have the run of the place," I said. "I don't think I have any rodents, but your cats can make sure. I'm going to put you in a room on the second floor. It's in the best shape of all of them."

We walked into the inn, and I pointed out the rooms of the main floor.

"This place is absolutely charming!" Missy said. "You said it needs lots of work, but I disagree."

"Wait until you spend a few hours here."

She glanced around, nostrils flaring as if sniffing the air.

"There's supernatural energy here," she said. "Lots of it."

"Yeah, my housemates. I have one ghost on the third floor, though I think there are more who haven't shown themselves yet. I have a gargoyle who hangs out in the front room here, but is known to pop up in unexpected places. And I have a vampire living in a crawlspace in the kitchen walls."

"A vampire living here?"

"Yes. Well, maybe not *living*, but residing. Since you're a home health nurse for elderly vampires, you won't mind Roderick. He's old and fairly agreeable. He basically came with the house."

"Yes. I work with vampires daily. Nightly, I mean. But I didn't think you'd be so nonchalant about him."

"He claims to have owned the building and disputes the foreclosure. He's been here for about a hundred and forty years, and there's no convincing him to leave. At least he promised to do all his hunting off the premises."

"Do you have a space where I can work with a magic circle?" Missy asked. "I'll draw it with a dry-erase marker, so it won't damage your floors."

"There's this room," I said, leading her into the front room. I had sent the large Oriental carpet out for cleaning, so there was plenty of room on the hardwood floor.

She glanced at the fireplace mantel.

"I can't concentrate with the gargoyles staring at me."

"Only the one on the far left is sentient. His name is Archibald, by the way."

"Hello, Archibald," she said. The stone figure didn't answer.

"Then how about in here?" I led her into the breakfast room.

"Perfect! Let's just move this table over a bit, and I'll be good."

We moved a table for four about three feet to the side, leaving her a space on the hardwood floor about eight feet wide.

"Let me feed the cats and set up their litter boxes, and we can get started. Back in a few," Missy said, striding quickly from the room.

I sat in a chair and stared out at the courtyard with its brick pavers surrounded by purple Bougainvillea and leafy palms, the small swimming pool at the far end. It was normally a serene scene that didn't ease my anxieties right now.

Because it still looked like a snowscape, thanks to a blizzard of bird poop. The rain yesterday hadn't washed it off fully.

Soon, Missy returned with a large, bulging tote bag that she set on the floor. She took a chair opposite me.

"Let's talk," she said, studying me as if I were one of her vampire or werewolf patients. "Has this witch or wizard or whatever he or she is, attacked you directly, inflicting pain, illness, or injury to your body?"

"No. So far, it's just been the birds. They tried to inflict all the above on me. But I had a shovel for self-protection. Unfortunately, there's still lots of bird poop all over the place, as you can see."

"I have an easy fix for that. It sounds like the birds were meant to intimidate you."

"I don't see what the point was," I said. "It wasn't like they were carrying little signs that said, 'Stop investigating Fathead.'"

"Fathead?"

"The guy I believe wants the coin."

"I would imagine the birds are only part of the battle plan. Anyway, I'm going to cast a spell to see if any hexes, spells, or curses have been placed upon you or the inn. So I need you to sit still and follow my instructions."

"I'm all yours."

Missy reached into her bag and pulled out a white dry-erase marker, then squatted on the floor and drew a large circle around herself. The white marker contrasted well with the dark, mahogany-colored floors that were nearly three centuries old. She drew a circle, about five feet in diameter, that was pretty close to perfect. She set five tea candles at equal points along the circumference of the circle and lit them with a lighter.

"First, some housekeeping," she said. She closed her eyes and murmured something in verse.

Rain poured into the courtyard. I hurried to the window. The sun was still out, and rain fell nowhere else but here. It was a heavy downpour, sending most of the white poop swirling away before the shower ended as abruptly as it had begun.

"Wow. Thank you," I said.

"Okay, now for the harder spell. Darla, try to relax. Take deep, slow breaths and clear your mind."

Missy did the same as she kneeled within the circle. She pulled a small cloth sack from her pocket and clutched it in her left hand, then closed her eyes. After a while, she chanted in what sounded like Latin.

Missy half opened her eyes and looked at me. I shut my eyes and pretended to be relaxing. More Latin chanting followed.

Then I smelled the waxy, burnt odor of extinguished candles. I opened my eyes to see that two of the candles had gone out.

"Just as I thought," Missy said. "You've been hexed. I can't identify the exact magic, but it's a surveillance spell of some sort."

"Surveillance?"

"To monitor what you're doing. Let's see if the spell is on you directly, or on the inn. Do me a favor and leave the house, walk about a block away. Wait a few minutes before you return."

So that's what I did. I walked down the street, past a rare open lot where a home had been knocked down years ago. I was secretly hoping to buy it to use for guest parking, but only if the inn turned out to be profitable.

I stood there among the weeds and overgrown grass. It freaked me out to think a witch or wizard was monitoring me. I felt violated.

When I returned to the inn, Missy looked at me with concern.

"The spell is attached to you," she said. "I felt it fade when you left. I don't like this, because it's much harder to put the spell on you than on a building or car. That's how they directed the enchanted birds to attack you—because the surveillance spell is attached to you and they always know your location."

"How exactly do they attach a spell to me?"

"They needed to have had direct personal contact with you. Or they have a possession of yours."

"That's creepy," I said, feeling angry. "Can they hear what I say? Can they watch me in the shower? Do they see me when I'm sleeping, like Santa? I snore at night. It's kind of embarrassing."

"Sorry, Darla, I don't know. It doesn't feel very powerful, so hopefully, it only knows where you are, not how loudly you snore."

"If this is the person who wants the coin, it's only a matter of time before they attack me and steal it."

"Our first step in fighting back is to nullify the spell. It will take me a long time to find how to disable it, but until then we can block it. I'll make you a charm to wear that will hinder the spell's ability to send information about you to the magician. Can I use your kitchen?"

"Sure. This one isn't fully equipped yet. You can use the one in my cottage if you need more gear."

"All I need is water, a pot, and a stove."

"Then this one will do."

Missy carried her tote bag into the kitchen.

I waited in the breakfast room, fretting over how the magician had put a spell on me and what he had learned about me. How long has this spell been on me? He would have seen everywhere I went, including the cemetery. He would know I'd been investigating Liszt.

I felt like I had eyes on me. I had an itch on my butt, but I didn't want to scratch it. What if I was being watched right at that moment? I hoped that wasn't the case, and all he knew was my location.

Missy screamed in the kitchen. It was more of a startled scream than a help-I'm-in-danger scream, but I rushed in, just in case.

"I apologize for upsetting you," Archibald said. He perched on the wall above the sink.

"You didn't upset me," Missy said. "I didn't know you were there. Actually, you weren't there when I came in here."

"Missy, meet Archibald. You'll get used to him," I said. "He pops up whenever and wherever he wants. I haven't seen him attached to drywall, though."

"Perish the thought," Archibald said. "Drywall! What a ridiculous, unsubstantial material."

Missy had stopped listening to him. She had a pot of water heating on the gas range and was removing vials and baggies from her tote bag. They contained strange-colored liquids, dried herbs, unidentifiable powders, and small objects that appeared flesh-based—something I didn't want to contemplate.

I decided it was best if I didn't watch whatever she was doing, so I returned to the breakfast room. About a half hour later, Missy joined me. She carried a small, black felt pouch.

"I have to cast another spell to activate this," she said.

Missy knelt within her magic circle and re-lit the candles. Low murmuring came from her. I heard what sounded like Latin and then a language I didn't recognize. She held the pouch cupped in her hands extended in front of her. More murmuring followed. It was making me sleepy.

Finally, Missy placed the pouch on the floor and rubbed her hand on the edge of the circle, erasing a few inches of it.

"The circle is broken, the spell has been cast, your amulet has been charged with power." She handed the pouch to me.

"Wear it around your neck or keep it in your pocket at all times, and you should be invisible to your enemy's surveillance spell."

"What about a shower?"

"You think I need one?" Missy asked, crinkling her nostrils.

"No, I meant what do I do with the amulet when I shower?"

"You should put it in a watertight bag. It must be in contact with your body at all times. If you don't want them to watch you shower."

I shuddered. "Got it."

While Missy wiped the circle from the floor and collected her materials, I thought out loud.

"So, if they're surveilling me, and sending birds to poop on me, do they know I have the coin?"

"My guess is they don't," Missy said. "If they did, they'd send another thug after you to steal it. I think they know you're investigating them and want to intimidate you. So, even if the birds weren't carrying little signs telling you to back off, that's what their poop and pecking were saying."

"What should I do next to protect myself?"

"Like I said before, I think they might have a possession of yours. You need to get it back."

CHAPTER 17
VAMPIRE THIEF

I was dreaming about Cory. It was one of those dreams in which you're quite aware that it's a dream and you're enjoying it so much you want it to never end. You see, it was a naughty dream. Cory and I were in the large claw-footed tub in our Key West bathroom. There were candles beside the tub, oils in the water, and soft music playing in the background.

You can imagine where this was going.

Beads of water glistened on Cory's lean chest. His straight brown hair was wet and nearly covered his eyes. He gave me a long, deep kiss that made me dizzy as I leaned back in the water.

But then the bathroom door opened.

And a dog padded in.

It was a German Shepherd, big and dark-brown. We didn't own a dog, let alone a German Shepherd.

"Isn't it time you moved on?" the dog asked.

It didn't seem odd for a dog to talk in a dream, but it had hijacked my naughty fantasy. As the author of my dream, I tried to steer it back to the original plot. But you know how dreams are: they never cooperate.

"There's someone in your house," the dog said.

"Shouldn't you go chase him off?" I asked.

"I'm not your guard dog."

I woke up, disappointed my dream was over. It made me miss Cory even more, even though I had been building calluses on my heart to protect it from the hurt.

A shush of wood as a drawer carefully slid open.

There *was* someone in my house. In my bedroom. My heart raced.

Pretending to still be asleep, I cracked open one eye. A man in black clothing stood at my dresser across from the foot of my bed. He was just a dark shadow, except for the white skin of his bald head. It was a stark, unnatural white.

The skin of a vampire?

Yeah, I sensed something unnatural about him, that he was not a living creature. I had nailed to my door the seal that had imprisoned Roderick in the crawlspace, hoping it would keep vampires out. The seal obviously didn't work anymore.

The vampire's head jerked around, and he studied me. He must have sensed I was awake. I closed my eyes and tried to act convincingly like an asleep person, but my heart was pounding so loudly I was afraid he could hear it.

The room was silent, except for my heart. I opened one eye to a slit.

The vampire stood at the end of my bed and smiled. One fang gleamed in the faint ambient light from the window. He held his hand palm out towards me and moved it in a circle. A wave of gray filled my mind, and the world went away.

THERE'S ANOTHER KIND OF SELF-AWARE DREAM WE ALL KNOW: the bad kind that we struggle to get out of. That's what I was experiencing after the vampire did whatever he did to me.

I was in a place between sleep and wakefulness, paralyzed in the gray haze. My breathing was slow, my heartbeat had calmed. It was almost a pleasant oblivion. Except my fear and helplessness weren't suppressed.

The vampire continued to search my room while I lay there unable to move. He systematically went through my dresser, the bedside tables, the closet, and the two unpacked boxes that still sat on the floor. He was very efficient and mostly silent, with the air of someone who did this kind of thing often.

He slid his hands between the mattress and the box spring, and I recoiled at the feel of his hands so near me, but I couldn't move.

After he left the room, faint sounds of his opening drawers and cabinets in the rest of my cottage reached me. I struggled harder now to break free from whatever he had done to me. I breathed faster and deeper and tried to clear my head. Any movement of my body was simply impossible.

Finally, he left the cottage. The screen door slammed shut despite how careful he had been.

Now, I really went nuts trying to get free. It was a maddening feeling, not just being drugged and half-asleep, but being unable to move. Practically hyperventilating, I moaned. The vibrations in my throat were reassuring. Next, I got my eyes to dart back and forth even though the lids were still sealed. My nose twitched.

Then I moved my toes. I was making progress. But the problem was, the vampire was inside the inn now. And I was desperate to prevent him from finding the coin, hidden inside a crack in the mortar in the interior of the front room's fireplace.

I had no confidence whatsoever that Archibald would or

could prevent the coin from being taken. I had begged him to raise an alarm if someone searched for it there, but that wouldn't do me any good right now.

My breathing became stronger and deeper. Each time my lungs filled, my chest felt looser and my shoulders more flexible. Soon, my fingers tingled, and I could move them slightly. Next, my wrists flexed.

I slid my right hand until it touched my upper thigh. I pinched myself until it hurt.

Boy, that was the best pain I'd ever felt.

I continued twitching and straining, finally moving my legs and reaching with my right arm to slap myself in the face. After the second slap, my eyes popped open. Groaning with the exertion, I pushed myself into a sitting position.

Soon, I would be able to get out of bed and walk into the inn. But how was I supposed to stop the vampire when I got there?

I STIFFLY CROSSED THE COURTYARD, ALMOST TRIPPING ON THE pavers. Instead of going directly inside, I stopped at a gardening shed hidden in the corner behind a clump of palms. I rooted around inside until I found something suitable.

A three-foot-long metal rod with a sharpened end used for staking immature shrubs. I needed it to stake a vampire.

What else was I supposed to do with the vampire? Ask him politely to leave? Hope he doesn't find the coin and gets too bored to stick around?

For a moment, I wondered if it was worth putting my life in danger trying to kill him. It's not as if I had hands-on experience doing that kind of thing. Maybe I should just let him take the stupid coin.

But, the person who wanted the coin was responsible for

Danielle's death. I would not allow them to win. Even if it required staking my first, and hopefully last, vampire.

I opened the door to the inn which went directly into the sitting room. There was only darkness and silence within.

How does one find a vampire?

Answer: very carefully.

I crept through the room, holding the metal stake like a spear. My eyes were well-adjusted to the dark, but nowhere near as sensitive as the vampire's would be. Anxiety forced me through the main hall to the front parlor with the fireplace where I had hidden the coin.

No one was there, and Archibald slept in stony silence. I was tempted to check on the coin, but that would give its location away if the vampire was spying on me. Maybe I should take the coin and run. But then I would forever be on the run.

Next, I checked the breakfast room. Shadows pooled beneath the small, round tables, but no one was in here. I hoped the creature wasn't upstairs. It would be much more difficult for me to find it among the bedrooms and almost impossible to take it by surprise. Plus, Missy was in 204, and I didn't want her in danger.

I peered into the kitchen, barely illuminated by the light on the restaurant-sized coffee maker. No one was in here, but I should probably—

A hand seized my neck and lifted me into the air, feet dangling. My windpipe was half choked off, making me wheeze as I panicked.

"What are you doing out of bed?" an unnatural, papery voice said.

"Looking for a snack," I tried to joke, but I barely could hear my words.

He knocked the stake from my hands.

"Did you truly think you could stick me with that? Such an outright display of hostility forces me to defend myself. I shall stick you with these."

He bared two long, sharp, yellowed fangs.

Then the smaller refrigerator jumped away from the wall and a dark figure shot across the room. A force like a truck hit the vampire, and he and I went flying. I landed on the floor against the cabinets.

I had a ringside seat to the pandemonium: two vampires fighting savagely, with movements so rapid they were a blur to this human's eyes.

One of them was Roderick. He had come to try to save me.

It was sort of like a dog fight, with all the snapping and snarling and the difficulty in figuring out what was going on. But this fight wasn't just on the kitchen floor; it was on the walls, the ceiling, and midair. My expensive copper pots that hung on the wall crashed to the floor.

Drops of blood spattered across the floor. I didn't know whose they were, since both vampires were only a blur to me. The fight appeared to consist of complicated maneuvers to get the other vampire into a death hold.

And that's exactly what happened to Roderick. The other vampire threw him onto his back upon the butcher-block island. He held Roderick's mouth closed with one hand and squeezed his throat with the other. He looked at me and hissed.

"Tell me where you've hidden the coin, or I tear out the throat of your guard dog and then eat his heart," he said in his dry, sloughing voice.

Roderick's eyes darted to mine. He was panicked.

I have to admit, it wasn't an easy call. I had no special affection with Roderick. He came with the inn, like an unfortunately designed bathroom addition. I feared he would cause future problems with guests. But I couldn't just allow him to die like this. And he had put himself in danger to save me, after all.

And refusing the intruder vampire's demands wouldn't mean he'd go away.

"The coin is hidden in the fireplace in the front parlor," I said.

The vampire disappeared from the kitchen so quickly, I didn't see him move.

"I am sorry you had to reveal the hiding place," Roderick said to me as he sat up on the butcher-block island. His face was bruised and scratched, but it healed in front of my eyes. "If you hadn't told him, he would have killed me and then tortured you until you relented."

"I thought that would be the case."

"San Marcos is notorious for its caste of vampire thieves. They are regulated by the vampire guild, the Guild of the Eternal Night, and sell their services to the highest bidder."

"In this case, it's the individual who has been stopping at nothing to find the coin," I said.

He nodded, rubbing his throat.

A sharp cry and sounds of a struggle came from the parlor.

I rushed out of the kitchen, Roderick shooting past me. When I reached the parlor, I stopped, mouth agape.

The vampire thief's head seemed to be affixed to the stone mantel of the fireplace. Archibald's impish arm encircled the vampire's neck in a rock-hard grip. The gargoyle had snared the thief and turned back into stone, making it impossible for the vampire to escape.

"Well done, Archibald," Roderick said.

"Release me," the thief whispered through his constricted windpipe. He was in an awkward position, forced to stand on tiptoe to keep from being strangled because of Archibald's high perch beneath the tall mantel.

"Why should we?" Roderick asked. "You were going to violate the Guild's code that forbids vampires from killing one of their kind."

"Only a threat," he choked out.

"So you say now. I believe a suitable punishment would be to keep you trapped there forever in hibernation. Or I could open the curtains so you will burn to death when the sun rises and floods the room. Technically, it would be the sun, and not I, that kills you."

"Mercy. I beg of you."

"If we release you, you must leave this property and never enter it again. You must obey this dictum under the vampire laws of territory. Do you understand?"

"Yes."

"Very well. Archibald, you may release him now."

"Wait," I said. "Who hired you?"

"I do not know," the vampire said. "We thieves never know. Only our Master accepts jobs and assigns thieves."

I nodded in resignation.

"Archibald. You may release him," Roderick said.

The gargoyle didn't respond.

"He only wakes up when he wants to," I said.

The trapped vampire whimpered.

"Archibald," Roderick said.

The stone gargoyle shimmered and then became flesh. His arm lowered the vampire to the floor and released him. Then he slapped him in the face.

I giggled, unable to help myself.

The vampire thief hissed with indignation. I blinked my eyes, and he was gone.

"Thank you, gentlemen, for helping me," I said.

"This inn has been a rather uneventful place for centuries,"

Archibald said. "It looks as if that won't be the case anymore, now that you've moved in."

"I guess not," I said. "At least not until I resolve this mystery behind the coin. It's getting out of control, and I have to find out who's responsible."

CHAPTER 18

THE KNEE BONE

Could the guy who wanted the coin be Fathead? I had originally thought he wanted the coin solely for its monetary value, which was more than I could imagine because of its rarity and the overlay of Aztec gold. But what if the guy who wanted it was a religious fanatic?

Maybe he knew about the soldiers, nearly 500 years ago, who saw the face of God while touching the coin. He could have heard the story somewhere buried in history books or legends. He could have wondered if the box and parchment found by an archeologist in a dig a few years ago were related to the coin he had heard about. If he had ordered it stolen, and read the Spaniard's letter about the men who had seen the face of God, he would know the coin had this power.

What if this person believed the coin would enable him, too, to view the face of God?

But that didn't make sense. The coin-seeker would need to have the ability of psychometry to see the Huguenot's vision. That's how the Spaniard who killed him saw it, through his own psychometric abilities. Maybe the coin-seeker didn't understand this or believed there was some other way to get the coin to work for him, through magic, say.

In other words, the guy was going to use his paranormal ability or supernatural means to obtain the vision from the coin. If not, would simply owning the coin be enough for him? Would he kill to get this coin just to own it, knowing the coin's power but unable to enjoy it himself?

Could be. Collectors were pretty fanatical sometimes. I had ordered and read the book that Liszt had in his bag, *Looting the Ancient World*. It described wealthy collectors who stopped at nothing to buy religious relics through the black market.

But there was one important fact not to forget: If the coin allowed you to see the face of God, it would be the last thing you saw. You would die, like the Spanish soldier who took the coin from the Frenchman.

It was time to ask questions. I began at a jewelry shop across the street from Danielle's shuttered shop. The store was called "A-Tisket, A-Tasket," and sold antique jewelry, watches, coins, and keepsakes. It was like Danielle's store, but less focused on coins. It also had less security. I walked right in with the tinkling of bells above the door.

"Hi, Connie, do you remember me? I'm Darla, a friend of Danielle's."

Before I left town for Key West, I used to stop by Danielle's store and Connie would often be there visiting.

"Yes, Darla, of course I remember you. I'm sorry for your loss."

"And I'm sorry for yours. That's why I'm here. If you haven't heard, the man who the police believe killed Danielle was himself killed in jail."

"He got what he deserved. Even if it wasn't through the justice system."

Connie was tall with gray hair worn straight. She had an

owlish face and reading glasses that hung from a lanyard around her neck. Her face was stern from grief and anger.

"The police think a prisoner on drugs did it," I said. "I'm not so sure. I believe the person who hired Danielle's killer ordered it. Someone who very badly wanted a Spanish coin Danielle had."

"How can I help you?" Connie asked.

"The person who hired him might be a collector of rare religious artifacts. Does any customer of yours come to mind?"

"I rarely sell high-end, rare items like Danielle did, but I've had some nice pieces over the years. Some religious items sit gathering dust for years, and others get snatched up the same day I put them on display. I confess I'm ignorant about why. I'm more passionate about antique timepieces myself. But I promise you, I'll go through my sales records and ask some of the other shop owners. Give me your number or email, and I'll let you know what I find out. Anything to bring justice for Danielle."

I thanked her and left the store. I randomly stopped at a few similar stores and asked about serious collectors, but didn't get any helpful answers.

But, as I wandered down Castile Street, past high-end art galleries, I came upon a doorway with a small brass sign. It was engraved with the name: Ancient City Auctioneers. I went inside.

There was a reception area and offices to the right. To the left was an open door to an empty auditorium.

"Can I assist you?" asked a well-dressed platinum blonde with an icy voice.

"Do you have any upcoming auctions that include antique religious icons?"

"We had one earlier this month. We don't expect another for quite some time."

"Is there a way to find out who some of the biggest buyers were? Just curious."

Yeah, just curious. By the skeptical look on her face, she knew I was full of it.

"Many of our buyers prefer to remain anonymous."

Yeah. That made sense. Especially if the buyer was a psycho.

Before I turned to leave, I had a thought: "Do you still have any of the programs from that auction?"

"There are a few on that table by the door."

"Do you mind if I take one?"

"Go right ahead," she said before returning her attention to her computer. She was done with me.

I picked up the expensive booklet, printed on thick, glossy paper, and left.

When I returned to my cottage, I flipped through the catalogue filled with photos and descriptions of the items that were to be auctioned. There were paintings of religious scenes and personages from different faiths, some dating to as early as Medieval times. There were statuettes and figurines of saints and prophets made with precious metals. Crosses, crucifixes, and rosaries were in abundance. There was even a small gold and silver reliquary purporting to contain a piece of bone from St. Theodore. Some starting bids were staggering—in the tens of thousands.

I opened my laptop to do internet searches for as many of the items as I had time for. You never knew what could pop up.

Some items yielded no results other than links to auction houses. Others didn't have specific enough information to do me any good. I learned a bit about sacred art, so it wasn't a total waste of time.

But when I searched for the reliquary of St. Theodore, I got lucky. There were lots of articles. One in particular caught my eye, because it was from our local newspaper.

"Carpet King Buys Saint's Knee Bone," the headline proclaimed.

The article included a photo of carpet and flooring magnate Norman Knobble posing in an expensive living room with the reliquary. He was awfully proud of it, said his very wide, self-satisfied grin.

The story described Knobble's collection of religious objects to be "massive." The Carpet King said he hoped to build a museum of religion in San Marcos and fill it with his collection. Knobble, the article said, was active in the Catholic Church and made a big point of his stores being closed on Sundays and on Good Friday. Knobble also had political aspirations, and was considering a run for governor.

My, my, I thought. Is this our guy? And look at that big, fat pumpkin of a head. Had I found "Fathead," the cemetery vandal? And does this confirm he was also the person trying to obtain the coin?

It seemed odd that the same person who hired a thug and then a vampire to steal the coin would also be involved with something as despicable, and petty, as smashing headstones. But it wasn't my job to psychoanalyze criminal dirtbags.

My next route was to scour the internet for information on Knobble. He didn't appear to have any social media accounts. I found a photo of him on a site for the fortieth reunion of his class from the local Catholic high school. I expected to find more society photos, since he was a prominent business owner, but he and his wife apparently didn't get out much. Most of the search results I got were links to the twelve locations of Knobble Family Flooring, the business founded by his late father.

When I concentrated on news articles, I had more luck. Lots of stories came up about his charitable donations to religious foundations and his contemplated entry into the governor's race. When I searched public records, there wasn't much.

What did catch my eye was activity under the name Knobble Ventures. The company had taken out lots of mortgages on properties downtown. I guessed he was playing around in real estate investing. Then one entry caught my eye, for 15 Prince Street.

It was the building that housed Danielle's store.

I remembered Jen had said a third party owned Danielle's store. Since Knobble owned the building, had he bought the store, too?

All of this made me really suspicious that Knobble was the guy I was looking for.

Since the spell was put on me after Liszt departed the earth, I assumed he had shared his suspicions of me with his employer without confirming I had the coin. The visit by the vampire thief meant the suspicions were very strong. In order to find out if Knobble was the guy seeking the coin, I decided to do something risky.

I called the main number of Knobble's company and asked to speak to him. They wouldn't let me, of course. The big man was not available. I asked to leave a message. They connected me to a general voicemail box. I left a message anyway.

"I have the coin that Mr. Knobble is looking for. I'll sell it for a reasonable offer. If he wants it, leave a post on your company's social media page."

So that was that. Nothing to do but wait and check their page frequently. I thought I had been pretty clever.

But after a day went by with no post on their page that I could construe as indicating an interest in my offer, I had to think of another strategy. Maybe I needed professional help. And I didn't mean of the psychiatric variety.

"Detective Samson, please," I asked the desk sergeant at the police station. Samson had agreed to meet with me, but I refused to mention details over the phone.

I didn't want to sit in one of the institutional hard-plastic chairs. A police station didn't attract the kind of crowd I wanted to share butt warmth with. I stood to the side and checked my phone like a restless teenager.

"Ms. Chesswick?"

I perked up at the sight of him. He wore a fishing shirt again.

"Thanks for seeing me," I said.

"Follow me."

He led me into a bullpen filled with desks. Only two other detectives were there, talking about sports. He gestured to a guest chair and sat down at his desk.

"Have you ever looked into Norman Knobble?" I asked, my voice low so I wouldn't be overheard.

"The Carpet King?"

I nodded.

"Why would I look into him?"

I noticed for the first time how blue Samson's eyes were. Um, what were we talking about?

"Knobble is a big collector of religious antiquities," I managed to say.

"So? What does that have to do with coins?"

"This isn't just any coin. It has religious significance. It has an overlay made with Aztec gold melted from an object associated with religious sacrifices. The coin is a religious icon."

"I won't ask how you found all that out. But you've got a gap in your trail connecting it to Knobble that's miles wide."

"There's a legend around the coin, that involves being able to see the face of God. The coin would be very attractive to a super-devout person. Knobble is very active in the Catholic Church."

"So are tens of thousands of people around here."

"He also has the means to pay people to find the coin for him."

"I'm sorry, but you're not convincing me the least bit."

"He owns the building that housed Danielle's gallery."

"Then why would he have someone kill her?"

"Can't you look into him, just in case?" I was afraid I sounded desperate.

"I'm not going to interview the guy for no reason. And I don't have time to chase down your hunches. I'm sorry."

"Can't you search records and stuff? Maybe his name will pop up associated with a related crime."

Samson leaned back in his chair and stared at me, deciding what to do. I wished he would turn those baby blues down a few degrees.

"I'll see if he has a record, and search for his name in our incident database," he said. "I'll only promise you a few minutes on this wild goose chase."

"Thank you." I gave my most electric smile.

But after I left the building, I had serious doubts Samson would be true to his word.

CHAPTER 19
UNFORTUNATE TIMING

I was drinking wine with Missy when Samson called. Actually, I was swigging from a glass of Cabernet Sauvignon in the foyer of the inn like a drunken sailor. The idea of having a nightly wine and cheese serving, once the inn was open, had come to me, and I suppose I was getting into the spirit of it. I imagined a table with a few wines and sherries to choose from, along with canapés and cheeses, to attract guests out of their rooms and encourage them to meet each other and chat. It would be a civilized version of Happy Hour.

That gave me the idea to pop a cork and bring the bottle into the foyer to imagine what the event would be like. Okay, the truth is, I'd been super stressed, and I just wanted to get drunk with my cousin, okay?

"You sound drunk," Samson said.

"I'm not quite drunk yet. Give me a few more minutes."

"It's Detective Samson," I whispered to Missy, my phone on mute.

"Well, the reason I'm calling is I ran Knobble's name through the system, and it popped up involving a federal investigation into antiquities smuggling."

"Really?"

"Yeah. Rare stone tablets illegally imported from Iraq. Archeological sites are looted all the time, and the items get sold on the black market."

Knobble wanted to open a museum about religion.

"That sounds like objects right out of the Old Testament," I said.

"If he's a collector of religious items, Iraq is like a candy shop. So, according to the records, he claims ignorance that the items left the country illegally. It's doubtful the Feds will charge him with anything. I wanted you to know I looked into him like I promised, and that's all I've got. I don't think this does anything to advance your theory that he's the one who's after the coin."

"It proves he's willing to break the law to get the items he wants."

"But not that he paid a thug to steal a coin from a dealer."

"I'm not trying to prove a case in court," I said.

"That's exactly what will ultimately have to happen if you want to punish this guy. And so far, I've seen no evidence that will stand up in court."

I tried to argue, but he cut me off.

"I'm sorry, Ms. Chesswick, but I have to go."

"You can call me Darla."

"I'm late for an appointment and have to wrap up things here before I go. Good night."

"He hung up on me," I said to Missy.

"Cops are busy."

"I really think this Knobble guy should be investigated, but Samson won't take me seriously. He wants more evidence.

Danielle is dead, and I was almost killed, and Samson doesn't seem to care."

"You know how cops are. They're not going to follow someone else's hunch."

"I'm going to talk to him face to face."

"You're drunk. You shouldn't be driving."

"Well, you're not drunk. And you will drive me."

My tone made it clear that I would not abide with any arguing. Soon, we were in Missy's ancient car for the short drive down dark side streets to the police station.

"I hope he's still there," I said.

"I hope he doesn't arrest you for public intoxication."

"Wine only makes me more charming."

The parking lots for the police station were behind the building. The visitors' lot was empty at this late hour. As we pulled in, I saw Samson exiting the building, hurrying through the employee lot.

"Let me out here," I said, almost falling as I jumped out before the car had fully stopped.

"Detective!" I called out as I tried to catch up with him.

He looked my way, but didn't stop. He reached a white pickup truck and climbed into the cab. I rushed to the driver's side door and knocked on his window.

"I need to talk, just for a moment," I said.

He lowered the window, but also started the engine.

"I'm sorry," he said. "I'm really late. I have to go now."

"I'll be quick. I wanted to explain why you should trust my gut feeling on Knobble."

He put the truck in reverse. "Please step back. I don't want to run over your foot."

I didn't believe I was drunk, but I obnoxiously refused to give in and let him go. I had my hands on the door so he couldn't roll up his window.

He looked at the sky with a fearful expression.

"I'm sorry. Please let me go," he said.

I looked at the sky, too. The moon was rising above the horizon. A full moon.

Samson groaned. And then, it happened.

Fur sprouted all over his face.

And, no, I wasn't seeing this through wine goggles. Fur really appeared and covered all his skin. On his hands and arms, too. He convulsed, then steadied himself. Something was odd about the shape of his jaw beneath all that fur. He convulsed again.

The pickup reversed quickly as I stepped backward.

"Do you really think you should be driving?" I called after him.

Despite his convulsions, he successfully exited the lot into the street and drove away. I returned to Missy's car.

"What happened?" she asked.

"You know how you can be attracted to a guy, and he turns out to be a beast?"

"All the time."

Samson called me the next morning.

"I'm really sorry about last night," he said.

"Did what I see happen really happen?"

"Yeah. That's why I was in such a hurry to get home."

"So, you're a werewolf?"

"You're very observant. You should consider going into law enforcement."

"I never saw a werewolf before. I didn't think they existed. But now that I'm back in San Marcos, I'm encountering a lot of things I never believed existed."

"Ms. Chesswick—"

"Darla."

"Darla, it's important that you keep last night secret. No one in San Marcos knows I'm a werewolf, except for other members of our guild. No one at the Police Department can find out, or my career is finished. Do you understand?"

"Sure." I liked the intimacy of a shared secret. Plus, it gave me some leverage over him.

"I became infected from a werewolf bite only two years ago," he said, "when I was camping in the Ocala National Forest. So I'm new at being a shifter. That's why I blew it last night. I got caught up in work and didn't leave early enough. You didn't help matters."

"Sorry. You know, I was thinking it's rather hypocritical of you to be such a skeptic about my psychic abilities. You're a supernatural, for crying out loud. Why are you so narrow-minded?"

"I'm not. I'm a cop. I'm naturally skeptical. Most people who claim they have paranormal abilities really don't. And those who have them, often don't understand their gifts. But I believe in your abilities. It still doesn't mean I trust other people's gut feelings."

"Well, I'm trusting mine right now."

"Fine. As soon as I see some evidence that a district attorney will respect, then I'll be on board."

It was at times like this that I didn't feel so guilty for not revealing that I had the coin. I was on my own in investigating Knobble. Fine.

"By the way, have you ever eaten anyone?" I asked.

"What?"

"As a werewolf. Have you ever eaten a human?"

"Of course not. I'm a cop. I don't murder people."

"What about animals?"

"Look, I've enjoyed hunting since I was a kid and hunted

with my dad. But I don't hunt anything when I've shifted. I only shift on the full moon, when I have no choice, and I fight the urge to go after prey. Just because I'm a werewolf doesn't mean I have to enjoy it."

And it didn't mean I had to enjoy knowing he was a werewolf. I had found him undeniably attractive, but now I was confused about how I felt. It was a bad idea to allow myself such feelings, anyway. He was a cop investigating the murder of my friend. And he'd probably bust me if he found out I had the coin.

"Okay, detective, I'll let you go now. Don't worry, I'll keep your secret."

"You can call me Mike."

"Thank you, detective."

As I clicked off, I remembered my dream the other night of the dog in my bathroom. Too weird.

I EXPLAINED TO MISSY WHAT I HAD LEARNED ABOUT SAMSON. She had no issue with werewolves, since many of her patients were shifters.

"Of course, all my werewolf patients are retired, old, and flabby," she said. "I wouldn't be attracted to them, whether or not they were werewolves. Those shifter romance novels, the ones that have shirtless guys with ripped abs on their covers, are nothing like real life. Do you really want a guy shedding fur all over your bedroom?"

"I didn't say I wanted to see Samson naked."

"No, but it's obvious you were thinking it. And you're the telepathic one, not me."

"I didn't realize I was being so obvious."

"I need to meet this guy."

"Look," I said, "Cory left me only a year ago. I'm not ready for another relationship. I don't even know if Samson is married or not. But listen to me! How pathetic! The thought that he was attractive crossed my mind a few times, that's all. I don't know how I got from that to the word 'relationship.'"

"You deserve to be with someone you love," Missy said.

"What about you? Is there someone in your life?"

"A friend or two. No romance. No burning desire to marry again. And I'm just fine."

"I don't have a burning desire either," I said. "For marriage, that is. Besides, what man would want all my baggage: this money pit of an inn and a daughter who takes whatever money is left?"

I thought about Samson and his secret. My knowing it definitely changed the equation. It would come in handy to have a police detective who wanted to stay on my good side.

CHAPTER 20

RECONNAISSANCE

Knobble's Carpet Kingdom had a dozen locations throughout Northeast and Central Florida. But their flagship store was in San Marcos, in the same neighborhood it had been since I was a little girl. In fact, my mom and dad had once gone there to try an ill-advised trend called shag carpeting for their bedrooms. Maybe that's why the name Knobble always had bad connotations for me.

When I had looked up the company to call Knobble, their corporate headquarters had the same address as their flagship store. When I drove there, I expected to find they'd added an office building to the property, but I was wrong. There was just the old, rambling warehouse store that had always stood there, expanding gradually throughout the years.

I backed into a parking spot near the exit from the lot, in case I needed to make a quick getaway. That was because I didn't have a plan other than to bluff my way into Knobble's office and see if any of my possessions were in there for creating the surveillance spell. I knew it was very unlikely. Or the possession in question could be something as generic as a ballpoint pen I wouldn't recognize as mine even if I saw it.

But what else was I to do? Breaking into Knobble's home was the other alternative, but I wasn't going to do that. Now that I knew the Vampire Guild had very accomplished thieves among their members, they would be Plan B.

I walked in the front door and before I could even get my bearings, a salesperson attached himself to me like a mosquito.

"Isn't it a lovely evening?" he asked. He had a big, black mustache and a shiny bald head. He was even shorter than me. "Are you looking for carpeting or flooring? We're running a special on wood veneer."

"Just browsing," I said.

"We also have a great selection of floor tile. Lots of people don't realize we sell tile, too."

"I don't know what I want yet. Just browsing today." I picked up my pace, trying to get away from him.

"You know what's big now?" He was matching me stride for stride. "Vinyl veneer. You can lay it on top of your old tiles without the cost of removing them."

I halted. He nearly collided with me.

"Where are the restrooms?" I asked. "I think I'm going to be sick."

"Go straight to the back of the store, turn left and go through the doors."

I left him behind and followed his directions. After passing through the doors into another wing of the building, I came upon an open door leading to bathrooms, but also a door leading to a suite of offices. The drone of a vacuum came from deep in its recesses.

It was late enough that I might find the offices empty. I walked into the suite purposefully, as if I knew what I was doing.

The offices I passed were crowded with old furniture, piles of boxes, and stacks of carpet samples. I went down the hallway to the very end. And there was a much larger office. On the wall above the desk, a large oil painting of Norman Knobble smiled down at me. I'd found my destination.

The office wasn't as cramped as the others. There was an enormous desk, a sitting area with a leather couch and chairs, a bureau to the side that held an ancient-looking gold crucifix in a glass case, and a really old Bible also inside a case. The room was neat and uncluttered. The desk was nearly bare except for a phone and an antique box.

I didn't see anything that could have been one of my possessions.

I chastised myself for being naïve enough to think it would be that easy. Even if my possession was here and not in another location, it would probably be locked in a drawer or cabinet. It was impractical and too risky to rummage through everything.

I went to the door and looked down the hallway. No one was around. The vacuum had stopped as well. Still, I needed to hurry.

I approached the desk and sat in Knobble's leather chair. It had tons of psychic energy simmering in it. I took deep breaths until I relaxed as much as possible under the circumstances. Then I placed my hands on the armrests.

Memories appeared. I browsed them until I found a vivid one. An image of the room. A woman standing behind me, massaging my shoulders. She was speaking—

— *"The letter you stole said whoever sees the face of God will die from the coin's curse. I'm not convinced the coin's curse kills you with magic directly. I think it's the power of suggestion. It affects someone with psychometric abilities, who experiences the death of someone else, in a profoundly powerful way. My theory is that a psychometric would most likely die from a cardiac arrest or brain aneurysm. So the spell I invented would work on the cardiovascular system to prevent that from happening."*

"You're convinced your spell is sufficient protection against the death curse?"

"I am. And my other spell will harvest the magic of the coin from the Aztec gold and the spells the Spanish wizard added. If the magic is as powerful as the rumors say, you will have an irresistible control over people."

My divine purpose is to be the shepherd of the flock and lead them away from sin and to redemption. An angel told me in a dream I should attain this through the political system. My future lies before me, as clear as the line running down the center of the highway.

I will become a powerful leader. Not through minor state and local offices. No, I will go big. I will become governor, and then President of the United States. From laminate flooring to the marble floors of the White House.

(A smile grows upon my face.) I don't just want to be president. I want to be the Supreme Leader, the most powerful one who ever ruled. And I will steer our sinful nation back to purity—

There were many more memories in this chair. But I didn't care about his loveless marriage, the little Knobbles who grew up to be loser trust-fund kids, or the family heritage of discount flooring. I needed more recent memories.

I had an idea. The phone, which Knobble surely touched every day, might tell me a thing or two.

I grasped the handset.

Nothing at first. Maybe the guy only used his cellphone. But soon words came into my head. They were indecipherable, just white noise of different voices like the burbling of a stream. Eventually, the noise grew louder, and I picked up conversation fragments of people from phone calls with Knobble.

I attempted Laurel's technique of not getting sucked into the memories, of remaining above them and skimming the surface. Hearing random conversations would be a waste of time. I wanted to find an important memory of Knobble's, something powerful or emotional. Something that told me what the man's purpose was.

Finally, there was something big. I sensed anger and frustration boiling over. It frightened me as I homed in on it, as I got closer and the anger vibrated in my chest and I lost my sense of control, plunging into the darkness of anger and hate. I—

—am tired of wasting time. I need the power now. We've already filed the paperwork for my candidacy and lined up donors. I need the power from the coin that was prophesied.

No, they're not just legends. I read the passage in Cortez' diary about the Aztec gold anointed with the sacrificial blood, the Spanish silver created by a legendary alchemist and enchanted by the grand wizard Lazaro. That coin was magical before it was filled with the vision of the face of God . . . yes, it was. How else did it end up back in Spanish hands after the French privateers stole it? Why else was that heretic holding it in his hands when he faced his death? Even the heretic sensed the power of it.

I need that power, and I need to see the face of God. No one deserves it more than me, who fights all the heretics and religious charlatans who have corrupted the True Christianity. Don't you realize what this will do for me? All this power and the knowledge of God's face? I'll win the governorship hands down. And then it's on to the presidency, and I'll have the entire country in my control to purify and punish and make pious like it should be. Do you finally understand my vision?

Liszt said he believes the friend of the coin dealer has the coin. Get it from her. Put her under surveillance. Kill her if you have to. Just say the word and I'll put a man on it. I know she has the coin, and I want it now. I said now. I don't care what you do to her. Conjure up another hydra if that's what it takes. But do it now—

—a disturbance. Snap out of it. Snap out of it, Darla!

Knobble was standing in his office doorway, his eyes fixed upon me.

Oops.

CHAPTER 21
FATHEAD

A fter the shock of seeing him, and the fear for myself, you know what my first thought was?

He really does have a fat head. The photo in the newspaper didn't do him justice. And the painting behind his desk proved the artist wisely took a detour from realism in order to please his client.

My next thought, which should have been my first, was: how do I get out of this?

"What are you doing in my office?" he asked with menace. He was a large, imposing guy who, although overweight, seemed strong for his early sixties.

"I'm with the cleaning service," I said. "Would you like your desk polished?"

He frowned and squinted his eyes. He didn't believe me. Then he suddenly moved toward me.

"Are you trying to steal something?"

"I was ordering a pizza. Sorry I used your phone."

I wasn't strong enough to get away if he grabbed me. But I was small and quick. I waited until he got close to the desk.

Then I feinted left and darted right. I circled around him and sprinted out the door.

"Security alert," Knobble's voice boomed over the intercom. "Lockdown. Subject is in the building."

What a paranoid dude, I thought. I had hoped to make it across the sales floor, but salespeople converged in my direction.

I ran past the bathrooms and collided with the guy who had approached me before.

"Hello! Did you find anything you're interested in?"

Feeling like a cornered rat, I desperately searched for an escape route.

A fire exit was at the end of the hall. Would they lock the fire exits? I'm sure it would be illegal, but that wouldn't stop Knobble. I ran to the door and threw my body against the hand bar.

It opened, thank God.

The fire alarm was deafening.

"Hey! Stop right there."

No, they didn't lock the fire exit. But they stationed a security guard outside of it.

Before I could move two steps, the big lunkhead had seized me by the upper arms.

"Let go of me," I said. "I'm not a shoplifter. You think I have a carpet roll or box of tiles hidden under my blouse?"

"Just following orders," he said, trying to avoid eye contact. Then his eyes shot toward the door I had exited.

Norman Knobble walked toward us. The alarm ceased at last.

"Nothing is missing from my office," he told the guard. "But hold her for a few more minutes."

He reached for my purse that was still clutched in my left hand. I couldn't move it away from him because the guard held my arms.

"You have no right to search my purse," I said.

He smiled. "I'm not going to search it."

I'm going to read it, his thought popped into my head.

Read it?

He placed three fingers on the leather handle, close to my hand, and closed his eyes.

Oh, no. I realized he was a psychometrist. Now his obsession with religious antiquities made sense. He was hoping to read the memories of the holy people who had handled them centuries ago. And the coin—he could experience what the Huguenot had. He would see the face of God. But wouldn't that kill him?

And, of course, he was reading my own memories. Such as the fact that I was afraid he would find out I was the one who now had the coin. Fortunately, it wasn't in my purse and my mind hadn't gone to where I'd hid it.

Whatever he learned, my telepathy didn't tell me. But his self-satisfied grin made me fear the worst.

"You can let her go now, Henry," Knobble said.

I shook my arms to get the blood flowing again and walked toward my car while I had my chance.

"It was nice meeting you, Ms. Chesswick," he said.

I shivered as I wondered what that creep had found out about me.

"THE WAR HAS BEGUN," I SAID TO MISSY WHEN I RETURNED to the inn. She was in a wingback chair in the sitting room reading a novel. "We have to get ready."

"I was hoping you were taking me to dinner tonight. San Marcos is supposed to have such good restaurants."

I froze. What kind of hostess was I? My cousin was bailing me out of a mess yet again, and I haven't fed her other than sandwiches at lunch?

I explained what had just happened with Knobble.

"Oh, my," she said. "Maybe it's not a good night for dining out."

"Not really. But definitely soon. On a night when I'm not expecting to be attacked. Tonight, I'll throw together something in my cottage."

"It will give us a chance to talk strategy and tactics," Missy said.

In the cottage, while I chopped garlic, basil, and onions for a simple marinara sauce, we went over the possible scenarios. The most likely one would involve thugs breaking into the inn and searching for the coin. If I was here, they'd beat and torture me until I gave up the coin's location. If I wasn't here, they'd find me, then beat and torture me.

"I don't like this scenario," I said.

A second scenario, a variation of the first, included Knobble coming along with his thugs to read my personal objects, hoping to find a memory of where I hid the coin. This placed Knobble at the crime scene. Since he had participated in the cemetery vandalism, he obviously didn't mind being reckless. Even with Knobble employing his paranormal gift, there would probably be some beating and torturing.

"That one's not much better," I said.

Missy suggested a third scenario.

"He, or someone employed by him, has magical abilities," she said. "So they could use a spell to find the coin. Then they could come here when no one was around and steal it, without all the extra potential criminal charges."

"At least there's no beating and torturing."

"Yes, and I can defend against it more easily. I have a spell that creates a blind zone around a hiding place. So any magic seeking to find it won't be able to pick up any data from the object it's seeking. This is a great spell because the other magician won't sense that a spell has even been activated."

"Sounds good to me."

After we finished the spaghetti meal, we returned to the main house.

"You need to tell me where the hiding place is," Missy said.

"Originally," I dropped my voice to a whisper, "I put it in the crawlspace in the wall where Roderick sleeps. It would be safe, at least during the day when he's there. But what about at night? And I don't completely trust him. He's too desperate for cash and might try to sell it. I decided on another spot. Follow me."

I led the way into the front room. It was shadowy in there, with only the lamp on the desk giving any light. I reached into the fireplace and touched the top of the space, just past the mantel.

"Then, I hid it in a little niche in the stonework right here. But I had to give up the location to the vampire thief. So where I ended up was in here," I pointed to a book on a side table in the sitting area.

"Perfect," Missy said. "Let me get to work."

I left the room to allow her to cast her spell in private. This was a good time to double-check all the locks on the property. It was suddenly obvious to me how vulnerable the inn was. There were so many points of entry, so many old doors and windows that could be forced open. Even though the wall to the court-yard was about eight feet tall, someone could easily climb over with some help. The cottage, where I slept, now seemed so tiny and frail.

I returned to the front room just as Missy was finishing the spell.

"What else can we do for safety?" I asked.

"I will put a protection spell over the inn. It's like a bubble that can't be penetrated, except, sometimes, by certain magic. If I sense a magician trying to break through, I can adjust the spell to compensate. The flaw of the spell is that I have to monitor it constantly and keep it from fading."

"Which is the story of everything at my age."

She smiled. "Is it okay to draw on the floor in this room? I need a magic circle for this spell. It requires a lot of power."

"No problem. I'll get out of your way."

The Latin words of her invocation seeped into the living room, where I was trying unsuccessfully to relax. I sat in darkness to allow me to look out the window. Every shadow that flitted across the courtyard from swaying palms made me jump.

A long time later, Missy found me in the darkened room and sat across from me.

"We also should take advantage of your telepathy," she said.

"I don't have full control over it. Occasionally, someone's thoughts pop into my head. Most of the time, they don't."

"You need to train yourself. Two experienced telepaths can have a complete conversation with each other. Someday you'll be able to do that. For right now, we need a way to communicate if we're separated and in danger."

"You're not telepathic, are you?" I asked.

"No, but I've been able to communicate that way with beings who have supernatural powers. A dragon, to be specific. His power allowed him to project his words into my head and to receive mine in his. I want to try a spell on you."

"I don't know. . ."

"The spell is harmless. It works with your paranormal abilities and enhances them. It should function the way the dragon's supernatural power did and hopefully allow you to project your words into my mind. You might also hear my thoughts better than you normally would. You'll be able to control your ability more."

"It sounds scary," I said. "I'm still getting used to my psychometric ability. Will your spell strengthen that, too?"

"I don't know. I'm trying to focus it on your telepathy. But come on, let's do this. It's for your safety."

I nodded. "Okay. I'm ready to get zapped."

"It's not a zap, Darla."

Missy put her right hand on top of my head and used her left to remove something from her pocket.

"What's that?" I asked.

"It's a talisman called the Red Dragon. This thing is heavy-duty. I use it sometimes to strengthen my powers for certain spells."

She gripped it tightly, and a feeling like an electrical shock passed from her hand into my head. It only lasted a second or two.

"You said you wouldn't zap me."

She wasn't listening. Her eyes were closed as she murmured words in Latin, and then some in Hebrew.

Surprisingly, I felt more energetic. My mind seemed sharper. Maybe I could use this instead of memory-enhancing vitamins as I grew older.

Missy removed her hand and returned the talisman to her pocket.

"Okay," she said, "let's give it a try. Say something to me using only your mind."

What do you want to talk about? I asked in my thoughts.

Missy smiled. *Let's talk about staying safe.* Her words appeared in my head as naturally as a normal conversation.

Wow. It worked.

I was considering giving the coin to Knobble. To just end the whole thing, I thought.

"Did you understand that?" I asked aloud. "It was kind of a long thought."

Keep going telepathically.

I realized giving him the coin wouldn't solve anything. He knows that I know he's behind Danielle's murder.

I paused for a moment to gather my strength so I could keep my focus.

And he intends to use the vision of God, and the power that comes with it, for an evil purpose. To have dominium over people.

Yes, you're doing the right thing. He must be stopped.

Missy's head suddenly snapped backwards, and her eyes opened in fear.

"The protection bubble," she said. "Someone is trying to breach it. Using black magic."

Great, I thought. They didn't waste any time coming after me.

Missy yanked the talisman from her pocket, held it with both hands, and murmured in a language I didn't recognize with her eyes closed. I sat frozen with fear. I didn't know what to do. The entire battle was in the realm of magic, and there was no way I could help.

Missy reacted as if she was punched in the chest. She groaned, then stood up and braced herself, leaning slightly forward. She grunted with exertion. Sweat ran down from her hairline. I was powerless to help her.

Missy shook her head, sweat flying. She kept reciting the strange language.

She gasped in despair.

And then, I saw three dark figures running across the court-yard toward us, as if they could see us in the darkness.

The French doors near my chair burst open with a crunching of splintered wood and broken glass.

CHAPTER 22
THE WORST SCENARIO

T wo men rushed into the room and pushed me up against the far wall. I immediately recognized the big, bearded lunkhead, the security guard from the carpet store. The other man, slender with a swimmer's physique and a shaved head, was also familiar. I realized I had seen him in the memory of one of the cemetery vandals, who had been looking at this man as they climbed the fence.

The lunkhead held a pistol to Missy's jaw. The vandal pushed his gun into my forehead hard enough to hurt.

"It's the short one," the lunkhead said to his partner. "You know why we're here," he said to me. "Give it up."

"What, pray tell?" I said, pretending to not be afraid.

The vandal pushed the barrel harder into my forehead. "The coin."

"Don't waste our time," the lunkhead said, "or we're gonna hurt you real bad. Give us the coin, or we'll kill you and get the coin, anyway."

"I believe this is Scenario One," I said to Missy. "The worst scenario."

The man grabbed my throat with his free hand and squeezed hard enough that I couldn't breathe. White spots swirled across my vision.

Cooperate, Missy's words came into my thoughts. *And stall for time. I'm going to try to put a sleep spell on them.*

He released my throat. I gasped for air.

"I'll get the coin," I said with a scratchy voice.

I considered leading him to the crawlspace in the wall and unleashing Roderick on him. Then again, what if Roderick was out hunting? What would I do, say I'm sorry that I forgot it wasn't in here?

Once these guys realized I was messing with them, they would move into the beating and torturing phase. Or they'd just kill me outright.

I glanced at Missy. Her eyes were closed, and her lips moved slightly. I hoped her spell was almost complete.

"It's in the front room," I said.

"Get it," the vandal said. "Let's go."

He yanked me by the hair away from the wall and pushed me toward the hallway. "Show me where it is."

As soon as I began walking, he came up against my back and wrapped one arm around my neck. He pushed his gun barrel into the top of my head.

"Let's go. Be a good girl."

I walked into the hallway and turned toward the front room. It was awkward going, with a guy a foot taller than me pressed up against my back. I moved down the hall as slowly as I could without arousing suspicion.

When was Missy's spell going to kick in?

Finally, we reached the front room with its single floor lamp burning.

"Where is it?" the guy asked.

"There." I pointed to the fireplace.

"Don't mess with me. Get it now."

His arm withdrew from my neck and he jabbed me in the back of my head with his pistol.

A loud thud came from the other room. It sounded like a large human body falling onto the floor. Snoring soon followed.

I turned. My assailant was looking behind him, in the direction of the living room. I was about to make a run for it, hoping to get out of the front door.

Suddenly the man's knees buckled, and he sank to the floor, curling up into the fetal position.

Missy's magic had worked.

I hurried into the sitting room, eager to give my cousin a big hug.

Instead, I had a rude shock. Two more people were in the room. Fathead Knobble himself. And a woman who looked familiar. She turned toward me.

It was Esmerelda. My ex's fiancée. What was she doing here? This made no sense.

"I knew there was a witch in here, and I knew it couldn't be you," Esmerelda said to me.

"What do you mean?" I asked. "How did you know there's a witch here?"

She looked at me like I was an idiot. I guess I was.

"Witches know these things," she said.

Many women claimed their ex was dating a witch. Now, I could claim it literally.

"Esmerelda, this is my cousin, Missy. Esmerelda is my ex-husband's fiancée. I realize now she's the one who made the birds poop all over me. She must have especially enjoyed that."

"You're using black magic," Missy said to her.

"How observant of you."

"Black magic is banned in San Marcos."

"The Guild's bark is worse than its bite," Esmerelda said. "They haven't bothered to stop me yet."

Knobble hadn't said anything yet. He moved through the room, touching every surface of the furniture with his hands. Stopping at the chair where I had been sitting, he leaned over and placed his hands on the armrests and closed his eyes, letting seconds pass. He opened his eyes, smiled, and straightened up.

"The coin is in the front room," he said. "You moved it from the fireplace because the vampire thief knew it was there. Now it's in a book on a side table."

It's tough to keep secrets from a psychometrist. There is no way to wipe away the memories you leave everywhere in your day-to-day existence.

"Let's go get it," he said to me. "If you don't help me, I just find it myself."

I didn't doubt that he could.

The thought that this smug jerk, who had caused Danielle to get killed, infuriated me. He didn't deserve to have the coin, especially since he was planning to use its power to con millions of people into voting for him. The coin should be in a museum, not in the grubby hands of this evil man.

I wished I could destroy it rather than give it to him.

When we reached the front room, he opened his suit coat to show me he had a handgun tucked into his waistband. Then he pushed me into the room.

There was nothing I could do except obey him, unless I was willing to die at his hands. I was a mother with a daughter who hadn't yet been able to stand on her own two feet. I couldn't let myself die over a coin.

I went to the sitting area in a corner with four chairs, a chess-board table, and two smaller side tables. One held a book of poems by Tennyson. I had cut a circular hole in some pages at the back of the book that held the coin snuggly. Sorry about that, Lord Alfred. I carefully worked the coin out of the hole and held it in my palm. I closed my fingers around it, steeling my mind to keep from being sucked into one of the many memories in the silver and gold.

I turned around to face Knobble. He looked at me with a such a desperate hunger, a mixture of greed and longing with a lust that was almost sexual. He looked disgusting. I hated him.

He reached out his hand.

"Give it to me," he said. "I've waited so long. Give it to me."

I lifted my hand that held the coin.

And then I popped the coin into my mouth.

His eyes widened with surprise, then fear.

His hand moved so fast I didn't see it before it struck my jaw. He intended to knock the coin out of my mouth.

Instead, I swallowed it.

Thus began the wildest trip I could ever imagine. No combination of psychedelic drugs or pharmaceuticals could match it. I had basically overdosed on a pill filled with magic and memories. And it could very well kill me.

I'M SURE YOUR FIRST QUESTION IS, COULD I READ MEMORIES with the inside of my esophagus rather than my fingers? The answer is yes, as I quickly learned. I guessed I could make the psychic connection if any part of my flesh touched an object, as long as shoes or thick clothing didn't get in the way.

With the coin lodged in my gullet, ever so slowly working its way down to my stomach, I picked up memories from Danielle when she hid the coin in her mouth from Liszt. Using the technique Laurel had taught me, I fought off the memories, resisted the connection, lifted my consciousness above the specific thoughts preserved in the energy in the coin.

I had to if I wanted to survive.

Knobble grabbed my upper arm and dragged me back to the living room. Missy was lying unconscious upon the floor, Esmerelda standing over her.

"What did you do to her?" I demanded.

"I showed her what a true sleeping spell is. And undid the ones she cast."

One of Knobble's goons, the lunkhead, stirred on the floor and sat up, still half asleep.

"This woman swallowed the coin," Knobble said angrily to Esmerelda.

"Are you serious?"

"Of course I am."

"That wasn't too bright," Esmerelda said. "Now I understand why she was dumb enough to marry Buddy."

"Hey!" I said, before wondering why I was about to defend the marriage from Hell.

"We have to cut her open and get the coin," Knobble said.

"Hey," I protested again. "Not so fast. I told the police that you'd be coming to attack me." It was a lie, but now I wish I had told them.

"Just be patient, Norman," Esmerelda said. "The coin will work its way through her, eventually."

CHAPTER 23
ANOTHER CHAPTER ABOUT BOWELS

"D o you have a laxative spell to, you know, hurry the process along?" Knobble asked.

"A laxative spell? I'm not some witch doctor," Esmerelda said, insulted. "I practice the rare art of black magic and necromancy. Summoning demons. Bringing corpses back to life. Not curing constipation."

"Okay, don't get upset. I was just asking. David," he said to the smaller goon who had entered the room after waking up from his involuntary nap. "Go to the drugstore and buy some laxatives. Henry," he said to the bigger goon, "get her into the van. We're taking her to a motel until this is over. Or until I lose my patience and gut her like a fish."

I wasn't sure how long it would take for the coin to work its way through my system, but I had to escape before then. I would not let this evil man get the coin.

Just then, a strange feeling came over me. Maybe the coin shifted as it descended in my esophagus. But I was overwhelmed with—

—heat and thirst. One barrel of drinking water had washed up on the beach. The other survivors and I quickly finished it after the arduous task of burying all the bodies of our drowned compatriots whom the surf carried ashore. Many more are still on the ocean floor, where the reef would be their grave.

I watch Morel and three surviving sailors float on a raft around the wreckage of the flotilla, searching for more supplies to salvage. In the low tide, the shattered hulls look like whale carcasses.

General Ribault, I'm so thankful he survived, is conferring with his officers. The men, who have been resting amongst the sea oats atop the dunes, are showing signs of activity. We all can sense that the order to march will come soon.

My clothing is almost dry, stiff with the ocean salt. God, I wish I had drinking water. I clasp in my hand my dearest possession that I had plucked from the spoils of the Spanish merchant ship we took a year ago. It wasn't in a sack of other coins, but in a box carrying jewelry and other valuables. It not only looked different with its overlay of gold, but I immediately sensed it was special. Almost as if it had power within it. Perhaps, it had been blessed by Providence.

Perhaps, it is why I was spared when so many others were not.

The drummer is signaling us to fall in. I pick up my arquebus, its match cord not yet dry, and line up with the surviving soldiers and sailors. There are two hundred of us at the most.

We wait until the drummer gives the signal to march, and the fifer begins my favorite marching song. The column of bedraggled men stretches ahead of me, moving north, the ocean to our right. We march just past the surf line where the sand is firmer, but marching on it is more tiring to my legs than solid ground.

I guess we will walk all the way back to Fort Caroline. If we don't starve to death first. I curse the gale that wrecked our fleet and—

—my head hit the inside wall of the van as it went over a bump. I was relieved to have snapped out of the Frenchman's memory. It was so strong and detailed. I understood the French that was spoken as if it were my native tongue. Because it was. I was the soldier. And if I had remained stuck in his memories, I would have experienced his death.

And died myself.

"Of course we're going to kill her," Esmerelda's voice said from the seat in front of me. "I just wanted to avoid the mess of butchering her. The guys can strangle or shoot her and dump the body somewhere. No muss, no fuss."

My heart fluttered with panic. Death by the Spaniards or by insane cultists.

Missy, can you help me? I called out with my mind.

No answer. Either my words never left my head, or never reached hers.

The van slowed. I peered into the darkness, trying to figure out where we were. There was nothing but woods, used car lots, lonely streetlamps. Nothing appeared familiar.

The van took a hard right into a parking lot with a neon sign for a motel. This must be where they were going to imprison me.

My intestinal tract gurgled. And then the feeling of vertigo swept over me. No, please don't make me—

—starve to death at this inlet. It was too wide and too deep to cross. Only the best swimmers would be able to make it. And to our west was a river and marshes. We couldn't get to Fort Caroline without a boat to cross this inlet.

Word runs through the troops that they have spotted men across the inlet. Spaniards. The forces of Menendez. Ribault's adjutant is waving a white flag.

The Spanish are waving a white flag in return! They will parley with us! The men are excited and relieved. If we must surrender to the Spanish, at least we won't die of hunger and thirst upon this beach.

One of our sailors, an excellent swimmer, dives into the water and swims toward the opposite shore, struggling against the current that wants to sweep him out to sea. A long column of pelicans glides by above him, curious at the sight. My throat is so dry, I—

—almost choked as someone forces a tablet of some sort into my mouth. I jerked my head away. I was lying on my back on a musty-smelling bed.

"Eat it!" the smaller goon tells me. "It won't harm you. It's just a laxative."

As much as I didn't want Knobble to get the coin, I also didn't want it inside me anymore. I couldn't control the visions and I was helpless as the Frenchman moved ever closer to his death. I couldn't wait to poop this coin out of me.

"I'll take it," I said, allowing the goon to slip the laxative into my mouth.

"And it's yummy chocolate-flavored! Here, you're supposed to take two."

I chewed on the tablets. They were not yummy.

The motel looked like it hadn't been updated since the seventies. Two queen-sized beds had bedspreads in a shade of mustard. The walls were yellow, too, and the owners hadn't bothered to hang a single picture. The furniture was dark brown. I dreaded seeing what the bathroom looked like, especially since the bathroom was the primary reason we were here.

Besides me, the two goons were the only people present. The big lunkhead sat on a chair by the window that was covered by heavy, dirty drapes. The smaller goon tossed the box of laxatives on the bedside table and sat on the other bed. Both were immersed in their phones. They were here only to keep me from escaping and wait until my digestive system did its magic.

Who would have to fish the coin out of the toilet? Maybe they would make me do it.

If they were planning on killing me anyway, I may as well flush the coin down the toilet. Yes, that was what I would do. It was a priceless, remarkable antiquity I hated to dispose of, but that was better than allowing Knobble to use it for evil.

My stomach ached. Was it from my anxiety or from the coin? Either way, take this as a lesson not to swallow rare coins. Or any coins. Because I—

—*try to resign myself to another night sleeping on the beach without food or water. The general and his council did not keep their voices low enough, and the soldiers overheard some of what they said. It spread amongst us like fire.*

After the negotiating party was ferried back to our side by a Spanish boat, they reported horrible tidings to the general. They saw the bodies of hundreds of Frenchmen, men from two other ships from our expeditionary fleet that had wrecked further north than we did and had reached this inlet a day before us. The Spaniards had executed them for being heretics in the eyes of Admiral Menendez.

The word had spread that Fort Caroline had been captured and every soldier of the garrison who was not Catholic had been put to the sword. When our negotiators asked for a ship to sail back to France, the Spaniards said they had none to spare. Their admiral was vague about whether we would meet the same fate as the fort's garrison and our soldiers on the other side of the inlet. When our negotiators offered money, Menendez seemed open to sparing our lives and taking us to their settlement as prisoners. But he wasn't definite.

Ribault and his officers had to decide if we would surrender the next day and risk whatever fate the Spanish decided for us. Or to remain here and starve to death.

Some men near me are weeping as we lie on the cold sand with no fires or any form of comfort. I stare at the stars above with my coin in hand and pray for mercy. If only—

—I could escape from this room, I thought, as I woke up from another overpowering vision that left me shaken. I was experiencing the pre-death terror of two people at once, and somehow, they both were me.

The smaller goon, David, wasn't in the room. No sounds came from the bathroom.

"Where's David?" I asked.

The bigger goon, I hadn't caught his name, looked up from the game he was playing on his phone.

"Went to get some food and coffee. Man, do you have that disease or syndrome that makes people fall asleep in the middle of anything?"

"It's called narcolepsy."

"Yeah, 'cause you'll just pass out suddenly, like really out. And you moan and talk to yourself."

"Then don't share a room with me on our next family vacation."

The lunkhead returned to his phone and ignored me. He had moved his chair closer to the door, the only way out of this place.

I brainstormed about ways to escape and came up empty. I could see nothing to attack him with. In motels like this, everything was bolted down so it couldn't be stolen. I didn't think suffocating him with a musty pillow would work.

Wait, what if there was an iron?

"I'm going to the bathroom," I said.

The lunkhead's face lit up with hope.

"No, not that kind. I need to go Number One."

He ignored me again. The sink and dressing area were open to the room and only the toilet and bathtub were behind a door. There was no closet, only a chrome assembly on the wall with hangers, towels, and . . . no ironing board or iron. In other words, no blunt-force weapon.

So I went into the bathroom and closed the door. It turned out that I needed to. There were no weapons in here, unless I thought I could disable the guy by shoving a tiny soap bar down his throat. I left the bathroom feeling defeated.

David was back. He was kind enough to bring a third coffee for me, along with delicious-looking donuts. I eyed them hungrily. Instead, David handed me a bran muffin.

"This is for you," he said. "Fiber is good for . . . you know."

I sighed and took a bite of the muffin.

Missy, can you hear me? Missy?

Was she still under the sleeping spell, or was a two-way telepathic conversation simply not going to work?

David's cellphone rang. He answered it, looked furtively at me, then quickly looked away.

"Nope, not yet. I'll let you know when. She's eating bran as we speak."

I felt a slight rumbling below. It was probably from the laxatives. Surely not from the bran. I put the muffin on the bedside table as a hot flash swept through me. Was that a menopausal hot flash? A symptom of intestinal distress? Or another—

—dawn with my mouth as dry as the sand. Dark clouds obscure the birth of the sun. Instead, far out to sea, bolts of lightning dance along the horizon. The men are awakening, but there is no food or water. There are no drums or fifes or trappings of martial ritual. A few orders are barked out, and men shuffle in an unorganized throng to the edge of the inlet where the Spanish longboat awaits with two oarsmen.

Ten of our men climb aboard and the boat rows across the choppy current to the other shore. We watch as a small group of Spanish soldiers hand our men ladles of water, wait for them to drink, and escort them away from the inlet, and up a tall sand dune. They disappear behind it.

The boat returns to our shore. Another ten men climb aboard. Along our march to the inlet, we had maintained discipline, organized by what was left of our companies. But now, we were just a starving, desperate mob anxious to learn our fate: mercy or death. Some men hang back, sensing our doom. I am one of them.

But as the boat makes its way back and forth, our number on this side of the inlet diminishes. Soon, it would be my turn.

The empty boat returns, its hull scratching upon the sand and seashells. The oarsmen get out and turn the boat around. Suddenly, the burly hand of Sergeant Alvarez seizes my shoulder and pushes me toward the boat. I climb aboard in the bow as nine men sit down behind me. The soldiers push us off the beach, and the oars dig into the water. I watch the far shore grow closer.

The wind shifts, coming from the north. I smell blood.

CHAPTER 24
HOT-SHEETS HOTEL

Missy's eyes fluttered open as the black-magic sleep spell faded. It wasn't as good as her own sleep spell, she noted with a bit of pride. She practiced white magic, based on the powers in herself and the energies of the earth. It was natural and pure. Black magic, in her opinion, was lazy and corrupt. It leveraged the supernatural powers of evil creatures, such as demons, and the energies of hatred and negation.

But that didn't change the fact that Esmerelda had beaten her. Missy had slept on the floor while they took Darla captive. Missy had to get to work fast.

Darla, can you hear me? she called with her mind. *Darla?*

No answer. She tried again, with no success. She worried Darla was trapped in a memory from the coin.

She clutched the Red Dragon talisman in her left hand. It immediately tingled as the power shot up her arm, through her heart, and into her head.

Darla, are you okay? Please answer me.

A single word popped into her head. It was in French. Missy

didn't know French except for some dirty words, and this was one of them.

Darla was trapped in the memories of someone who spoke French. There may have been more than one who had held the coin over the centuries, but Missy feared it was the French soldier, the one who had been executed. And Darla said that a psychometrist who experienced his death would die, too.

Darla, wake up! Snap out of it!

Missy didn't understand enough about psychometry to awaken Darla from her trance, other than shaking her body awake. She needed to find her cousin quickly.

She had spells to find people and large objects like vehicles. If the object of her search might be far away, the spells were laborious and lengthy. But, if she was confident the target was, say, within the same town, a newer spell she had learned would work more efficiently.

First, she needed an item that Darla used a lot or cherished. She would have to search in the guest cottage. As she stood up from the floor and brushed off her jeans, Darla's phone caught her eye on the end table next to where Darla had been sitting before the criminals broke in. This would do nicely.

Missy drew a magic circle on the floor, in the same place she had previously. She lit five candles placed along the circle's circumference and then knelt within. She recited the words of the spell and assembled an intense ball of energy within her, drawing upon earth, wind, fire, water, and spirit.

And then she focused on Darla's spiritual essence contained on and in the phone. For someone like Darla, who had the power of psychometry, this essence would provide the memories of the person who left it. Missy didn't have this ability, and for her, the essence had a different function. Her spell electrified the psychic essence. It appeared before her as a small glowing orb floating in the air above the phone.

"Find Darla," she commanded.

The orb zipped across the room and out of sight. Just like the opposite poles of magnets attract each other, the orb was drawn to the rest of Darla's spiritual essence, seeking to rejoin it. In other words, it sought Darla herself.

Missy fell into a semi-trance and waited. Eventually, a vision appeared to her. A run-down, two-story motel on a rural road near the interstate highway. The orb drew closer, trying to reach Darla, but Missy slowed it down so she could memorize what the motel looked like.

As the orb moved toward the building, Missy was lucky and got a look at the sign. The business was called the "Dreamy Inn."

The orb moved closer and passed into a room 113 on the first floor. Darla was lying on one of two beds, the one farthest from the door. Her eyes were closed, and her head twisted like she was having a nightmare. The orb flew invisibly over the heads of the two thugs who were guarding her and disappeared into Darla.

The vision ended. But now Missy had what she needed. After a quick internet search, she found where the motel was.

Before she drove to the motel, she enlisted a great power to help her rescue her cousin. It wasn't a spell or charm. She called 9-1-1 and reported that Darla had been kidnapped and was being held at the motel.

SHERIFF'S DEPUTY LOOPIS WAS DOUBTFUL ABOUT THIS assignment. When the dispatcher told him which motel, he recognized the name as a notorious destination for cheating spouses and ladies of the night. It didn't help that his backup, Deputy Blowfler, made a joke about the "hot-sheets hotel" the moment he pulled up.

Deputy Loopis was not prepared to encounter the man who opened the door to Room 113.

"You're the Carpet King!" Loopis said.

"I am," said the tall man, who obviously wore a rug of his own. "Is there a problem?"

"There was a report of a kidnapping. A woman."

"Officers, I hope you can sympathize with me," the Carpet King said. "I'm a married man, but I'm here with a very good friend."

Loopis and Blowfler exchanged knowing glances.

"Her ex is probably trying to get us in trouble by making false calls to 9-1-1," the great man said.

"I understand, sir," Loopis said. "We just want to make sure she isn't being held here against her will."

To Loopis' surprise, the King opened the door wider. A woman was sleeping atop the far bed. She looked like she was okay. Loopis wondered why a man as rich as the Carpet King didn't shell out the bucks for a nicer motel for his shenanigans.

"Looks like she had one too many drinks," the Carpet King said. "Now, as a married man with a public image, I hope you two gentlemen will be kind enough to show some discretion."

"I understand, sir," Loopis said. "We're sorry to bother you."

"You're just doing your jobs. I thank you for your service."

"We should have asked for a discount on laminate flooring," Blowfler said as they returned to their cruisers.

"Dang it, you're right."

THE TWO OARSMEN PULL HARD, PLOWING THE BOAT ACROSS THE current in the inlet, the boat low in the water with the weight of the ten passengers. Spray hits my face as I sit in the bow. I'm so thirsty I'm

tempted to open my mouth and let the saltwater in, but I resist. They promised us water on the other side.

When we arrive on the opposite shore, a detachment of Spanish soldiers armed with pikes offer their hands to help us from the boat. Two stand at a distance, their arquebuses trained upon us. A Spaniard with a bucket and ladle gives us water. I drink it greedily, spilling some down my chin. It is delightful, but nowhere near enough.

An officer, the white plumage of a local bird stuffed in the band of his hat, approaches us.

He addresses us in French: "In the name of King Philip, rightful ruler of these lands whose sovereignty you violate, we take you as prisoners. Follow me."

He walked on the beach to a path that led through the sand dunes. Ahead, the dunes had risen into a hill, covered with sea oats and other vegetation. We climb it and I struggle, my body weak from hunger. As we descend on the other side, I am shocked by what I see.

Rows of Spaniards in body armor stand at attention, hidden by the hill from the view of those at the inlet.

And just to the north of them, lay scores of dead bodies. Our fellow French soldiers. It was true, then, that they had been executed.

Jacques, standing beside me, utters a curse under his breath.

"Prisoners," the Spanish officer says, "you must now confess to your faith. Who among you are Lutheran heretics, and who are true Christians?"

"I am a Catholic," Jacques says. And it was true.

"Go sit over there," the officer says, pointing to a spot at the foot of the hill where about a dozen Frenchmen sit, including the young drummer and fifer.

"The rest of you will march to San Marcos, where you will be held for ransom from your king. You must submit to have your hands bound, for I can spare only a few guards to escort you."

I remove the coin from my pocket and grip it in my right hand. I resolve to never let go of it, even after my last breath.

None of us resist as the Spaniards move among us, roughly tying our hands behind us with cords.

Helplessness spreads through me as soon as I lose the use of my hands. The smell of blood is heavy in the air. I know I will never reach San Marcos. My time on earth is about to end.

"March," the officer says.

He leads us past the rows of troops on a path well trampled in the sand by hundreds of feet, past clumps of coarse grass and small cacti. Up ahead, there is a line drawn across the path.

On the other side of the line, the sand is soaked with blood. Ten Spaniards armed with broadswords stand at attention.

Oh merciful God, please show me your love and mercy. Please grant me the sight of your face to show me the way to Heaven.

My fellow prisoners slow down. The pikemen prod us. The iron tip of one pricks my thigh. Pain snaps me out of my heavenly thoughts and brings back the physical fear.

I don't want to die.

One of our men is weeping behind me, I know not who. I want to weep, too. But I won't allow the Spaniards to see that.

I grasp the coin more tightly. Somehow, it brings me comfort. I've always known it was special, something about the golden layer atop the Spanish silver, covering the face of their ugly king, something about the golden Aztec symbols in the gold. They bring holiness to this coin.

As a Huguenot, I do not believe in religious idols. Worshipping statues of saints and crucifixes is idolatry and wrong. But this coin is different. I don't worship it. It simply brings the love of Christ to me and comforts—

—sharp pain in my lower stomach. But thank goodness for it, because it broke me free of the memory. I knew the French soldier was close to being executed on the sand. So close that my heart was racing here in the motel room, my adrenaline flooding my system.

And something was going on in my large intestine.

"She's awake," said Knobble. He and Esmerelda were in the room now, along with the two goons. It was quite claustrophobic in this tiny room.

"I know you are psychometric," he said to me. "Were you connecting with the coin after swallowing it?"

"Yes, and I was close to dying," I said.

"You mean being executed. You know about the coin's history, then?"

"Yes, and I know that someone with psychometry, who tries to read the victim's memories up to the point of death and seeing the face of God, will die, too."

"I don't know how much I believe that story," Knobble said. "So the Spaniard who took the coin afterwards died, but it could have been natural causes."

"I know you have the gift," I said. "Are you planning on gambling with your life when you read this coin?"

He smiled. "I think gambling is wicked. And I leave nothing to chance. Esmerelda has a spell that will protect me."

"Sounds far-fetched to me."

"But isn't the legend of this coin more far-fetched than that? But now that you've experienced the memories, that's not the case, no?"

"My stomach hurts," I said. "I think I overdosed on laxatives."

"It's the bran muffin," David said.

"Both of you, wait outside," Knobble said to his goons. They quickly obeyed.

"Go to the bathroom," Esmerelda said. "I will go with you, so you don't do anything stupid. And I disconnected the chain in the tank so you can't flush the toilet."

There went my plan to deny Knobble his coin.

I'll spare you the details of how uncomfortable it was having to go to the bathroom while being watched. But I was relieved when I felt—

—a fat raindrop hit my bare head. Then more splashed upon my head and shoulders. I raise my head and open my mouth, savoring the three or four drops that land on my parched tongue. I look at the dark clouds and pray to God that my death will be fast and painless.

My compatriots and I walk across the line in the sand into the blood-drenched killing zone.

CHAPTER 25
BLACK MAGIC

Missy arrived at the Dreamy Inn just as the two Sheriff's Department cars were leaving. The lights were on in Room 113, and the two thugs were standing outside the door.

In other words, the deputies had not rescued Darla.

Missy had to think fast. She was only one person against four, and one of those practiced black magic. Missy wasn't the kind of witch who cast spells that blew things up. Her occupation was a home-health nurse for elderly supernaturals. Healing was her thing, not fighting.

But Darla had to be rescued fast. Before Knobble and his witch did something horrible to her. Or before she died, along with the French soldier. She'd have to make up her battle plan along the way.

The first, and easiest, step was to neutralize the two guards. Missy's sleep spell had worked effectively before on these guys. She parked her car and cast a protection spell over herself. It hadn't been enough to prevent Esmerelda from breaching it at the inn, but sealing off a large property was difficult. Covering herself alone, it should at least hamper any attack spells the black magician threw at her if she was there tonight.

Missy got out of her car and strolled across the parking lot, directly toward Room 113. The men noticed her and looked up. She kept walking up to them, mouthing the words to the spell, grasping the talisman in her left hand.

"Hey, where do you think you're going?" the bigger thug asked.

"I'm coming to say goodnight. Sleep well."

Both men's eyes rolled up into their heads, their knees buckled, and they dropped to the concrete floor of the covered breezeway.

Missy stepped over them. The door to the room was locked, of course. Complex locks could be challenging for her, but this one was a very simple bolt mechanism. She cast a quick spell, and the lock slid open.

She opened the door only slightly and peered inside. Knobble was standing at the back of the room, staring at where the bathroom would be.

He turned and saw her.

Oh, my, Missy thought. She hadn't worked out her plan past this point.

"Esmerelda," Knobble said.

Missy quickly began casting a sleep spell. But it was too late.

Esmerelda stepped out of the bathroom and pointed her hand, palm outwards, toward Missy. Unseen hands threw Missy into the wall, almost knocking the wind out of her.

From Esmerelda's other hand came a violent force that bounced off Missy's protection bubble.

Esmerelda glanced back at the bathroom impatiently. Darla must be in there, Missy thought, and something might be wrong.

Eager to finish with Missy, Esmerelda flung both hands at

her. Missy felt as if a tight cord bound her, holding her to the wall.

"Hurry," Knobble said. "I think she's about to die. She needs to pass the coin. Can't you do something?"

Esmerelda opened a purse that was on the desk and removed a small chunk of stone, a piece of a coquina-rock wall.

"I'll try the same pooping spell I used for the bird attack."

Darla's agonizing moan came from the bathroom.

"Do it now," Knobble said.

WE STEP OVER THE LINE IN THE SAND. THE SPANISH OFFICER directs us to march to the left, and as soon as we turn, I detect movement behind us.

Jean exchanges a glance with me.

And he drops to the ground.

Screams erupt from all around me as my compatriots fall to their knees.

Icy cold steel plunges into my lower back. I, too, drop to my knees. I hold the sacred coin tightly in my hand while the swordsman looms above me, lifting his broadsword for the coup de grâce.

As the blood pours down my back, I feel my life ebbing. My vision blurs. Streaks of celestial light fill my eyes.

Oh merciful God, grant me a view of your heavenly face before I die. And then—

—the clink of metal hitting the toilet bowl. I wake up, freed of a burden both literal and metaphysical.

I'm also embarrassed to be sitting on the toilet in front of two people who aren't doctors or family.

"Excuse me while I tidy up," I said.

They ignored me.

"Get the coin out," Esmerelda said.

"You get it out! I'm the boss. I pay you to do my dirty work, even when it's really dirty."

I slipped past them out of the bathroom.

Wait, why was Missy standing like a mummy against the wall?

"Fancy meeting you here," I said.

"And where do you think *you're* going?" Esmerelda said to me.

Suddenly I was up against the wall, next to Missy, bound by something invisible and tight. I could barely breathe.

Esmerelda went into the bathroom. Soon the toilet flushed, and water in the sink ran for a very long time. Knobble stood in the doorway, eagerly awaiting his prize.

Finally, Esmerelda handed the coin to Knobble. He held it in both hands, almost as if afraid of it. His lips quivered with emotion.

"I've searched for this for years," he said. "My word, the power in it is intense. Even without the Huguenot's memories, this thing is loaded with those of many other people. And the pagan blood of the Aztecs. It's like a magical history book."

He went to the bed where I had been lying and sat down, placing the coin on the bedspread.

"I started picking up too many memories," he said. "I have to focus."

"You're not going to do that here, are you?" Esmerelda asked.

"I've waited too long for this coin. I don't want even the slightest chance of losing it. And, besides, I paid for the room."

"Are you sure you want to do this?"

"I need to see the face of my Lord. I need the power this will give me. *Now.* This is the new beginning for me, and for God's law to rule upon the earth. The war against the heretics must begin now."

Esmerelda sighed in exasperation.

"Hold on. I need to prepare the spell to protect you."

"Please, hurry," Knobble said like an impatient child.

"You can't rush black magic. I have to do this properly."

Esmerelda withdrew items from her purse. She crouched down and drew a large circle on the carpet with chalk outside the bathroom. Inside the circle, she drew a pentagram, but, unlike Missy's, this was an inverted one. She lit a black tea candle that she placed on the tip of the pentagram at the bottom of the circle.

Then, she took a small dagger and approached Knobble on the bed.

"You know the drill," she said.

He held out his hand, and she sliced his thumb, rubbing his blood on the dagger blade. She returned to the circle and Knobble sucked on his thumb like the petulant child he was.

Esmerelda knelt inside the circle, intoning words in a language I didn't recognize. She rested her head on the floor and rocked back and forth on her knees.

Suddenly, she sat up and placed the bloody dagger blade in the candle's flame. An acrid smell filled the room. The flame grew as if she'd added gasoline.

"You can proceed now," she said.

Knobble grabbed the coin, lifted his legs onto the bed, and leaned back against the headboard. The hand that held the coin rested in his lap. He closed his eyes.

He was silent for a while until he began moaning.

"The ship is breaking apart upon the reef. The cracking of the timbers is so loud. Water rushing in. Men are screaming."

He was quiet for a moment.

"No, no, I'm too far in advance. I need to move closer to the end."

He was silent again. But after a few minutes, he spoke.

"I am climbing out of the boat onto the beach on the other side of the inlet."

"I went through this myself," I whispered to Missy. "He's getting close to the execution. We need to stop him."

"How?" Missy asked. "I'm working to undo the spell that binds us, but then we'll have to tackle him and pry the coin from his hand. I don't know if we'll pull that off."

"Can you undo the spell that Esmerelda just cast, the one that protects him?"

"I think so. But won't that mean he'll die?"

"We don't know for sure. But I do know you'll be saving countless lives by preventing him from gaining power."

"We are marching through the dunes," Knobble said in a low voice. "I see so many Spanish troops. Up ahead, a line is drawn in the sand. There are swordsmen waiting beside the bloody sand. This is the scene of the slaughter."

"Please," I whispered to Missy.

MISSY HAD SUCCESSFULLY UNDONE THE SPELLS OF OTHERS before. It wasn't easy to nullify magic, especially black magic, but it was possible. Magic is simply different forms of energy that affect the physical world. Magic can move objects, alter matter, affect time, and more. But it depends upon properly focused energy properly applied and maintained.

Spells are more than magic words and rituals; they are constructed by the magician using energy like building blocks. Some spells are of simple construction, but the more powerful spells require a complex structure. And the more complex they are, the more vulnerable they are. By damaging certain parts of the structure, they can fall apart like in a game of Jenga. It required tremendous experience to do so, but Missy had grown a lot as a witch in both her knowledge and power.

Using her own magic, Missy sensed Esmerelda's spell and

studied it. The spell was powerful and drew upon dark energies emanating from Hell. It wasn't orderly like Missy's spells, but chaotic and messy, dark and dangerous.

She examined it, looking for a weakness, something like a block of wood that could be pulled out causing the entire structure to collapse upon itself.

"I am stepping over the line," Knobble intoned. "Let the killing begin and for my Lord to smile upon me."

Time was about to run out. The black magic was so convoluted that Missy was losing hope of defeating it. She clenched her jaw and focused harder, drawing more of her own energies to make her vision keener.

"The pain!" Knobble cried. "Slay me now!"

And then she spotted it: dark tendrils of hate and evil woven together like threads. They held the entire thing together.

She grasped the talisman in her pocket and as its power coursed through her, she severed the tendrils with a sharp thrust of her mind.

The flood of evil energy rushed over her like a wave, with the anguished wails of souls in Hell. And soon, it subsided.

The black-magic spell meant to protect Knobble was broken.

Esmerelda whimpered on the floor, crouched over her knees. Missy quickly cast a sleep spell over her, while she was in the trance-like state. Missy couldn't afford to sustain a black magic attack while still constrained by the binding spell.

"My life is slipping away as the swordsman prepares to kill me," Knobble said. "And now it's here! A vision of the Almighty! The light blinds me like a thousand suns. And God's face—I see it! It's, wait . . . how can this be so?

"Burning eyes of molten lava, the stench of sulfur. Long curved horns. The face of a goat? This is not God! God, where are you? Why am I . . . spinning. . ."

Knobble sagged on the bed, his head drooping sideways.

Then he slipped sideways, his head knocking the cheap lamp from the bedside table.

KNOBBLE WAS DEAD. I COULD TELL JUST BY LOOKING AT HIM. Missy, tied up by Esmerelda's Missy, tied up by Esmerelda's spell, panted beside me. A tear rolled down her cheek. She shouldn't have to feel responsible for Knobble's death. It was his own hubris that caused it.

Esmerelda was sleeping on the floor within her magic circle. Missy must have taken care of her, too.

"Missy, you did it!" I said.

She merely nodded.

"You saved the day. Maybe even saved the world. At the very least, you saved us from getting the worst governor ever. And this state has had some doozies."

Missy managed a smile.

"Don't feel badly about what happened," I said. "The good far outweighs the fact that he died. Like I said, you saved lives he would have led to being lost."

"I know," Missy said, softly.

"Now, if you could only free us from this binding spell, I would give you the biggest hug ever."

CHAPTER 26
GREAT BALLS OF FIRE

Missy was exhausted and disconsolate as I helped her from the motel room. But out in the fresh air, she seemed to perk up a little.

"You should ride with me back to the inn," I said.

"No, I don't want to leave my car here."

"No offense, but your car would not be at the top of a car thief's wish list," I said, glancing at the Toyota that was nearly old enough to have been driven by Spanish conquistadors.

She sighed and got in my passenger seat as I called 9-1-1. I reported a fatality, possibly a cardiac arrest. Then I called Detective Samson, and told him the object Liszt had killed Danielle for, the coin, was in the room.

"Maybe you'll have better luck with nine-one-one than I did when I called them to save you," Missy said.

"You did?"

"The officers were leaving the motel when I arrived."

"Knobble must have talked his way out of it. What are we going to do about Esmerelda? Is she under a sleeping spell?"

"Yes. I'll cancel the spell once the first responders get here. I don't think they'd be able to wake her up otherwise. Shouldn't we report her to the police? You said you believe she's the one who killed your friend's murderer with magic."

"But who is going to believe that? What I'll do is report her to the Magic Guild, and they'll punish her or force her out of town. And maybe I'll casually mention to my ex-husband that deputies found her in a motel with another man." I smiled at the thought of it.

"She's still a threat, you realize."

"She doesn't need the coin. What does she want from me?"

"Revenge," Missy said. "Her benefactor is dead, and another witch defeated her."

I brooded on that as I drove back to town.

Before we returned to the inn, we stopped for Cuban coffees at a late-night cafe away from the tourists.

"Well, once again, you've saved my butt, cousin," I said, enjoying the sharp smell of the coffee playing off the briny scent of the nearby bay. "How will I ever repay you?"

"No need," Missy said, smiling. "We're family. And aside from sharing blood, we share the gift of the paranormal."

"Sometimes I wonder if it's a gift or a burden."

"It's both. That's why we help each other out with no obligation to repay."

"Oh, I'll find a way to repay you. Whether you like it or not."

Before we left the cafe, Missy had a faraway look in her eyes.

"I hope you're not troubled by what happened tonight," I said.

"I'm a nurse, and I practice white magic. I shouldn't be causing death."

"Remember, you didn't kill him. He knowingly put himself in death's hands, hoping it would give him an unfair influence over others. And he was relying on evil magic to allow him to get away with it. Black magic is forbidden in this city. You did the right thing."

"Thank you for saying that. Maybe someday I'll believe you."

When we returned to the inn, I climbed the stairs with Missy to her room on the second floor, bringing a fresh set of bath towels. When we reached the landing, I stopped.

"That shouldn't be there," I said.

"What?"

"See that trapdoor on the ceiling?"

"For the attic?" she asked.

"Yes. But there are two problems. First, there can't be an attic here. There's a floor of rooms above it. Second, there's been a little issue here with the attic. It seems the door to it keeps disappearing and reappearing in other places."

"Oh, my." Missy looked at me strangely.

"One time, it appeared as a door in the hall, instead of a trap-door. I opened it, and went up some stairs that I never knew existed in this house. But near the top, I was overcome with dizziness and anxiety, so I never made it into the attic. Then, later, the door and stairs were gone."

"Oh, my," Missy said again. "It sounds like a gateway to the In Between."

"The what?"

"The In Between is a different plane of existence apart from the one we inhabit. Spirits of the dead who have not made it to Heaven or Hell spend time there. But living creatures can also visit. I've been there briefly twice. I wouldn't recommend it."

"But what does that have to do with the attic?"

"The gateways from earth to the In Between are always moving. It sounds like you have one appearing in your house disguised as an attic. Are you certain this house actually has an attic?"

"Um, I don't think it does."

"You want my advice? Don't go through any door to an attic in this inn. Because you might end up in the In Between and not be able to return."

"Okay," I said slowly, having difficulty processing this information. "Well, at least that means one less place to accumulate junk. That's sort of a problem with my family."

"Glad I could help."

I left the towels with Missy and said goodnight, thanking her once more for rescuing me from Knobble.

I SLEPT LIKE A ROCK THAT NIGHT. THAT IS, UNTIL THE explosions.

No, not gunshots. Not a car backfiring. Explosions. Coming from inside my inn. I threw on a T-shirt and shorts in my cottage and ran across the courtyard in the dark to the main building.

Great splashes of light came from upstairs. I fearfully crept up the stairs to a level from which I could see the second floor.

The door to Missy's room was open, and light poured out after each of the loud bangs. It sounded like a cannon from the fort was in there firing shots to entertain the tourists.

"Um, everything okay in there?" I asked.

"Not exactly," Missy replied. "I'm under magic attack. I—"

Another explosion.

"I'm trying to fight it off, unsuccessfully. It has to be Esmerelda."

"What can I do to help?"

"Try to find her. She must be nearby, close enough to have the inn in her line of sight."

"Got it," I said, retreating downstairs.

What, exactly, was I supposed to do with Esmerelda if I

found her? I didn't have a gun, but if I did, even Florida's lax gun laws wouldn't allow me to shoot her for performing magic. Burglars you could shoot. Magicians, no. Missionaries, no. Mountebanks, no. Mimes, maybe, but I needed to check on that.

So I grabbed the only weapon I could find, a fireplace poker leaning against the stone beneath a sleeping Archibald. And I ran outside into the pre-dawn darkness.

Now remember, it was magic causing the explosions in Missy's room. That means there weren't flaming balls flying at the inn like in a Medieval siege. There was nothing giving away Esmerelda's position. But I had an idea.

I touched the outside doorknob of the door leading to the front room. I sensed no recent energy indicating someone had tried to open it.

Next, I went around the corner to the main entrance on the side of the building. Had she checked if this door was locked? I touched the handle, and bingo! I immediately sensed—

—*it's locked. If I can't get to her, I need another tactic. Ah, I know! I'll incinerate the nasty witch. I need to find which floor she's on and get on the roof of one of those buildings*—

—The vision disappeared. Esmerelda must have let go of the handle.

I looked around at the neighboring buildings. Victorian homes lined Cadiz Street opposite the entrance. Across Hidalgo Avenue, in front of the inn, were newer, two-story brick town-homes. How would she get onto the roof of a private residence? Maybe she had black-magic techniques of leaping two stories in the air. But that wouldn't help me.

I walked along the front of the inn with increasing panic. Bursts of light filled the windows of Missy's room. I wondered how she was preventing herself from being incinerated. And there was the huge probability that the inn would catch fire. I had to hurry.

At the east side of the inn was an alley. On the other side of it was another historic Spanish Colonial home, but even older than mine. The "Oldest House" was owned by the Historical Society, which conducted tours there. Along the alley behind it sat a single-family home that was not a likely prospect.

The Oldest House was my best bet. But where, exactly, was she? Keeping to the shadows, I walked around the ancient building. The two-story structure had a sloped roof with no place on it to hide. So she had to be inside or on a second-floor balcony.

Using the cover of a giant Live Oak tree, I darted to the side of the house and looked for a way to enter, keeping close to the walls of the building to stay out of the trajectory of her vision. Similar to my inn, the Oldest House was a compound comprised of the main house and two smaller structures enclosing a court-yard. I was certain she was in the main house that faced mine.

I wondered what sort of magic Esmerelda had used to gain entry until I spotted it: a non-magical aluminum extension ladder. It leaned against the back of the house beneath an open second-story window with a broken pane. One would think the house had a burglar alarm, but presumably, the windows upstairs didn't have alarm sensors.

I hated climbing ladders. That's what husbands were for. But I tucked the fireplace poker into the belt of my jeans and began my ascent.

And boy, did I feel vulnerable. If Esmerelda heard me, she only had to push the ladder off the house as if from a castle wall, and I would be history. But I made it to the window and climbed in undetected. The witch must have been too preoccupied trying to kill my cousin.

It was difficult making my way in the dark through the rooms filled with historical exhibits. I stubbed my toe on a seventeenth-century chair that made a frightfully loud scraping sound on the wooden floor. I stopped and held my breath. No one came to investigate, thankfully.

I moved to the side of the floor that faced my house. There was no sign of Esmerelda near any windows. But then a dark silhouette moved across an open door.

She was on the balcony directly in front of me. She made exaggerated movements like she was pantomiming a player throwing a baseball. But the explosive fireballs she hurled at Missy's room were invisible and only materialized when they landed in her room.

Missy, I said mentally, *I found Esmerelda. She's in the Oldest House Museum, just east of the inn. Second floor. Use the ladder behind the house.*

I hoped my words actually left my head and reached Missy.

So what was my plan, now? Rush Esmerelda and beat her into submission with the fireplace poker? Yep, that's all I could think to do.

So rush her I did. I ran across the room brandishing the poker, entering the balcony. She turned her head and saw me, just as I swung the poker with all my might.

And a massive blast of air knocked me backwards into the room from which I had come, dropping me on my butt.

Esmerelda returned to her impression of a mime pitching baseballs.

With no smarter plan, I rushed her again. This time, I didn't even make it onto the balcony before the blast of wind knocked me backwards again.

My hair must be a mess.

Then the words popped into my head. Missy's words:

Distract her from her attack long enough for me to counterattack.

How? I asked in my mind.

Missy didn't answer. She was too busy fending off fireballs. I guessed it was up to me to find a distraction.

I clapped my hands loudly. No, that wasn't going to do the trick. Esmerelda wasn't a dog.

What could I do? Well, I only had one weapon, aside from the poker: my natural obnoxiousness.

"Aren't you getting tired of that, Esmerelda? Your magic isn't working. Missy's been completely unhurt by your silly fireballs. And to be quite honest, you look ridiculous. Like you're in some second-rate acting workshop."

If I bothered her, she didn't show it. I had no choice but to press on and dial up the obnoxiousness.

"It was very generous of you to take up with a loser like Buddy," I called to her. "After I dumped him, I didn't think anyone else would be as stupid as I was. Does he still eat potato chips in bed? That's the only thing he's good at doing in bed. I guess you don't care, because you're more interested in the fat old carpet salesman with a toupee. Who's too cheap to stay in a decent hotel. And didn't even leave his wife for you, even after you committed murder for him, killing a defenseless man in jail."

She pretended to ignore me, but seemed to be holding herself a bit more stiffly out of annoyance. I tried to dial up my obnoxiousness.

"But I suppose the carpet salesman was your only ticket to wealth," I continued, "since your quote-unquote event planning business was such a sham. I heard you're lucky if you book one event a month. Yeah, word gets around in a small city like this. So who are you going to sleep with next, now that the Carpet Crook is dead?"

"Shut up!" she screamed at me.

"Your magic failed him. That's why he's dead. And your magic won't let you get revenge on Missy. No, it's only going to land you in jail. Oh, you think the police can't connect you to the death because they don't believe in witchcraft? Think again. You'll end up spending your nights behind bars with a bunch of other losers like yourself. At least you'll look better in a jail jumpsuit than in those horrible colors you're—"

Her fashion sense. It was the straw that broke the camel's back. She charged at me like a zombie hungry for my brain. She tackled me and punched me in the face over and over.

I tried to get out from beneath her, but she was much bigger. I could have used that as an insult, but it was too late now.

I wrestled my way from under her and punched her in the forehead. My hand hurt. I got to my feet and looked for the poker. It lay on the floor behind me. As I went for it, I suddenly froze.

And I mean that, literally. Esmerelda must have zapped me with some magic, because I was paralyzed, stuck in my pose of reaching toward the poker. It was as if I had been turned into stone.

"Now who's the one who looks like a mime?" Esmerelda said. "And you shouldn't talk about colors. You and your mother dress yourselves from a Sears catalog from the 1970s. And I should add that I'm not regarded as the town kook like your mother is. And you, too."

I thought of a couple of witty rejoinders, but my mouth was as rigid as the non-Archibald gargoyles above my fireplace.

"It's because of you and your witch cousin that Norman died. You don't deserve to live. I'm going to turn your internal organs to stone."

She turned and returned to the balcony. Ah, that was where her magic circle was. I happened to have been immobilized with a view of what she was up to: kneeling within the circle, chanting, slicing her thumb with a dagger.

A chair thudded over in the other room. Probably the seventeenth-century one that I had tripped upon. Footsteps approached behind me. I couldn't turn my head to see who it was.

Esmerelda looked up in alarm at whoever was behind me. She spat out a swear word.

"I don't know a turn-to-stone spell, but this binding spell is pretty handy," said a familiar voice.

It was Missy's.

Esmerelda, deep into the spell-making process that was about to send me to my doom, couldn't react quickly enough. Missy uttered some words in Latin, and Esmerelda seized up and dropped prone on the floor. She spasmed, as if struggling against an invisible rope that bound her arms to her body and her legs together.

"I also have another handy spell," Missy said. "It makes you tell the truth. A black magician like yourself doesn't value the truth, but I do."

She approached Esmerelda, intoned a verse, then sprinkled a powder on her adversary. Next, she took out her phone, pointed it, and began shooting video.

"Did you kill Dennis Liszt in the county jail?" Missy demanded.

"Yes, I did. I summoned a demon that killed him."

"Were you just now attempting to burn me to death and kill Darla, too?"

"Yes, I was. And I will."

"No, you won't."

Missy turned to me. I was shocked to see that much of her hair had burned off, along with spots on her clothing. She went about casting another spell, probably the same one she had used to undo Esmerelda's spell in the motel room.

Before long, my muscles relaxed, and I could move again. I had the urge to kick Esmerelda in the face, but I resisted.

Esmerelda shook her head, as if trying to clear it of cobwebs.

"How long will your spells last on her?" I asked Missy.

"It looks like the truth spell is already fading, but we have the incriminating admissions we need to put her away. The binding spell should last for as long as I feed energy into it."

Yeah, the truth spell had faded for sure. Esmerelda stared at Missy with such hatred I wouldn't be surprised to see lasers shoot from her eyes. I didn't have the confidence my cousin had, that this black-magic witch was beaten.

So I tried to read her thoughts. As I've told you, my telepathy is sketchy. But tonight, it was working:

. . . the Hellfire spell is working, and the binding is almost burned away. Let her think I'm still bound, and then I'll hit her with a fireball right between the eyes . . . and then an immolation spell . . . almost ready . . .

My heart raced when I realized what she was going to do to Missy.

"I need to have a word with you," I said to my cousin.

"Can it wait? I'm concentrating on maintaining my spell."

I caught her eye and she realized how serious I was. Placing a hand on her shoulder, I led her to the side of the room, then whispered in her ear the thoughts I had just heard.

Missy's eyes widened into saucers. She recited a quick verse in Latin and waved her hand toward Esmerelda. The evil witch's eyes closed, and her body went limp on the floor.

"I didn't put a sleep spell on her before, because I wanted to use the truth spell," Missy explained. "I didn't realize she could overcome the binding spell so easily. You just saved my life. And yours, too."

"It was the least I could do. I still feel like I owe you."

"Nope. We're even, cousin. But let's wrap this up. Call your detective friend. Ask him to come here and arrest this woman."

"He's not exactly a friend," I said. But I called him up, and he actually answered, promising to arrive soon.

226

"He won't believe the part about the demon. But the burns on you tell the truth," I said.

"And wait until you see my room at the inn."

Wonderful, I thought. Cleaning the remaining bird poop had been a massive task. Now I had to repair burn damage.

No one ever talks about how costly the paranormal can be.

CHAPTER 27
HOMEWORK COMPLETED

There was finally an opportunity for the dinner out that I had promised Missy. We ate at The Wharf, a seafood restaurant built on pilings above the water in the city marina. This was where Sophie worked, and she hugged Missy with delight, but couldn't talk much since we weren't at one of her tables. The place was a bit overpriced and overly touristy, but the food was decent. I had the Florida lobster tails with a key-lime butter sauce, and Missy had the freshly caught Cobia.

"Again, you've bailed me out, cousin," I said.

"Actually, if you hadn't found Esmerelda and distracted her, then read her mind, I wouldn't be here tonight. I was running out of ways to fend off her fireball attacks. I think we make a wonderful team together. Here's to future collaborations," she said, offering her wine glass.

I clinked it with mine. "Hopefully, our next collaboration won't involve life and death."

"Good evening ladies," said a familiar male voice. "Long time, no see."

It was the werewolf detective standing before our table. Samson wore a black sports coat over a white dress shirt. It was a far cry from his usual fishing shirt.

"I didn't know this was your kind of place, detective," I said.

"You can call me Mike. I'm off duty, after all. This place was not my idea. It was my date's."

I had to admit I felt a little disappointed to hear the word, "date." But only a little, mind you.

"I thought you were married, detective," I said.

"Long divorced," he said, holding up a ringless hand.

She is looking hot tonight, he thought, his words appearing in my head.

But he's on a date, I reminded myself.

"I imagine your date wouldn't be pleased to see you chatting with two women."

He laughed. "She can't see me from our table. I noticed you two on my way back from the restroom. I'll let y'all enjoy your meal."

"Wait," Missy said. "Can you tell me anything about Esmerelda's status?"

"The prosecutor will press charges," he replied. "Right now, she's being held with no bond. She's not going anywhere for a while."

"Thank you," Missy said.

"I'll keep Ms. Chesswick apprised of the situation."

"Darla," I said.

He smiled. "Have a wonderful evening, ladies."

After he walked away, Missy said, "I think he likes you. He's kind of cute, in a rugged way. What do you think?"

"I've failed in two marriages. I don't trust my judgement much anymore."

"Sometimes, it takes a bit of practice before you get it right."

"Spoken by a woman who had only one marriage before hanging up her spurs."

"We'll see," Missy said. "But let's ask for the check. I need to get back tomorrow in time for patient visits in the evening, so I want to be on the road early. Well, early for someone who lives on vampire time."

On the way out, I stole a look at Samson's date. She was taller, younger, and prettier than me, at least in my harshly self-critical assessment.

But I didn't care. Right?

AFTER MISSY LEFT THE NEXT DAY, MY NAME WAS CALLED FROM the front room. Archibald had something to say.

"Laurel conveyed your report on the cemetery vandalism to the Guild, and I'm afraid to say we graded it as incomplete," the gargoyle said from beneath the fireplace mantel.

"What's wrong with it?"

"You theorized that the ringleader was motivated out of some blind hatred of Protestants. The Guild decided your conclusion was too simplistic. Especially given what you later learned about Norman Knobble."

"Well, he did believe Protestantism was illegitimate."

"Miss Darla, the Guild's mission is not just to preserve history, but to encourage truth and accuracy. You have some more investigating to do."

I sighed. How was I supposed to learn more? I was almost arrested for sneaking around in Knobble's office. And I definitely wasn't going to break into his home and touch every single possession, hoping to find a memory of the cemetery vandalism. All I could think of was to return to the scene of the crime.

So there I was, running my hands along the cast-iron fence where the vandals climbed over.

"Mommy, what is that lady doing?" a young girl said from behind me.

"She's a blind woman trying to find the gate. Or she's crazy. Let's keep walking."

I found the memories the vandals had left before they climbed over the fence. I double checked every inch of fence in the vicinity, but found no additional memories.

I entered the cemetery and walked to the family gravesite of Vincent Moulton. Workers had put the toppled obelisk back in place. The broken headstones were not repaired; the pieces were piled atop the bases like primitive cairns. There were probably no funds to put the pieces back together again.

I hadn't found any memories of value when I was here before, but I tried again, especially with Moulton's own headstone. It was the larger of the three. It would have received the most attention from the vandals. I touched the uppermost segment of stone where his name was carved. I ran my hands along the chiseled letters and—

—*Fathead keeps barking orders at me. I can't crack the dead guy's name in half, so I turn the piece over to put the name side on the ground. He's yelling at me to take the two sledgehammers and throw them in the river. But they're brand new. I bought them at the hardware store just today. I could use one of them at home, bust up the concrete slab where the shed used to be. You know, those bushes under that big oak there outside the fence, I could stash it there and come back for it tomorrow. Okay, okay, I hear you, Fathead, I'm doing it—*

—maybe, just maybe, I thought. What are the odds this guy didn't return for the sledgehammer, or a groundskeeper didn't find it? Pretty low, but I kept the image of the oak tree fresh from his memory and saw where it was. The tall tree with its long, curvy limbs creating plenty of shade over a thick growth of ivy. I left the cemetery and headed straight for it.

I was a little reluctant to root around in the ivy. What if snakes were in there? But I poked around with my foot, and before long it hit something hard. I kicked it toward me. It was heavy.

Sure enough, it was a large, two-handed sledgehammer, its handle the light color of new wood. What were the odds that Knobble had held it himself? Again, they were pretty slim. I crouched and touched the handle. It had a dark energy on it that was very familiar. I grasped the handle and felt it—

—jolt in my hands as the steel head hit the gravestone. Again and again I swing and smash the sledgehammer against the granite or whatever kind of stone this stupid philosopher's family bought for him, the airy-fairy, shallow-thinking fraud. Transcendentalism—what nonsense! I wasted all those semesters rhapsodizing about nature and sensuality and free will and nonsense. Pure nonsense. I should have been reading Thomas Aquinas instead of that drivel. Instead of letting my hair grow long and smoking dope and treating Professor Idiot like a prophet, letting him spoon feed me all the nonsense that Moulton wrote. And how I let my heart get crushed by Heather, that lying, no-good hippy. Swing harder! Break this stone! Make sure that Moulton spends eternity in the obscurity he deserves. Him and all those Protestant heretics. It feels so good to do this, along with the other thefts and vandalism. I can single-handedly wipe out the legacy of the heretics in this city. I—

—snapped out of it. Well, I felt both lucky and disappointed. Lucky that the sledgehammer was still here, and that I had found it. And disappointed that Knobble's motivation for vandalizing the grave was so petty and pitiful. But the fact that he had gone to the trouble to do it, and apparently was behind the other attacks on Protestant history, showed how dangerous a man he was. That he would commit all this destruction because of a decades-old, ridiculous grudge was ominous. Imagine what he would have done about his grudges if he had achieved high office and had the tools and resources of government at his disposal.

But his thirst for power caused him to overreach, to eat the forbidden fruit, so to speak. He had risked death to gain frightening power, and it was only a failed spell that prevented him from achieving it. A failure that allowed the death, he had paid to prevent, to catch him after all.

When I returned home, I revised my original report on the vandalism and emailed it to Laurel. I wondered how the Memory Guild archived all the facts and memories they maintained. In books? On computer servers? On scrolls? One day, I hoped to find out. In the meantime, I was happy to have contributed to them.

Speaking of archiving, there was a large storage closet on the ground floor of the inn where I decided to store some of my personal items. I had a half dozen boxes of old books, vinyl record albums, and mementos that I couldn't bear to throw out. The two closets in the cottage were too tiny. And there wasn't really an attic atop the inn.

I carried the boxes one by one into the inn and placed them in the back of the closet. Once the inn was running, this space would most likely start filling up with supplies and such, making access to the boxes difficult. So I looked inside each one, taking mental inventory of their contents.

When I got to the last box, which held Cory's mahogany box, I had a thought: now that I had discovered my strange gift of psychometry, why not use it for my own benefit? I could see what memories Cory's eyeglasses held, since he had been wearing them while reading on the night he walked out.

Was I prepared to be hurt all over again? Could I handle the cruel thoughts he may have had about me before he got up and walked out the door? Did I really want to see myself as he saw me when he realized he didn't want to look at me anymore?

Well, not really. But I needed to know. And after escaping death so recently, was I really too much of a wimp to face unkind thoughts, even if they were brutal?

I grabbed the mahogany box and sat down with it in my lap. I opened it. Inside was the magnifying glass and his eyeglasses, with thin wire frames that were no longer in fashion. Were these flimsy frames even capable of holding much psychic energy? If so, there would be years of memories in them. I needed to select only the most recent and vivid. I picked them up and—

—need to rest my eyes for a moment. (I remove my glasses and hold them in my left hand as I rub my eyes with my right.) The typeface of this book is too small. Small type, cheap paper. How appropriate for pulp fiction. Shallow characters, too, and—what the? Why are there three doors in the wall? Or have there always been three doors? Three identical white doors with the same rectangular panels, all closed. Bathroom, door to the guest bedroom, and closet. We have a closet in this room? Of course we do, moron, you're looking right at it. This is a small room, and that wall has always consisted mostly of doors. So, it's okay to be confused. Bathroom, guest room, closet. But what is in that closet? It probably has linens or things you never deal with, so you never go in there. Even so, I shouldn't be questioning it. Maybe I'm going senile. Look, there's only one way to settle this. Let's see what's behind Door Number Three—

—and the memory ended as he placed his glasses on the table as he stood up from his chair.

My stomach dropped as I remembered that there were only two doors in that wall. There was no closet in that room. The third door didn't exist.

My God, what if it was like the randomly appearing and disappearing of the attic doors in this inn? Would that mean it was a doorway to the In Between?

I wasn't fully convinced that there was an In Between. But if Missy was correct, and the In Between existed, and these disappearing doorways were portals through which you could disappear and not return . . .

Is that what happened to Cory? He went to check out what he thought was a closet door and disappeared into another plane of existence?

It sounded absolutely crazy. Complete nonsense. Impossible to believe.

But, I wanted to believe it. Because it would mean that Cory hadn't left me voluntarily. He was lost somewhere and hadn't been able to make it back to me. Lost for nearly a year.

Maybe he was dead. Surely, he must be. Missy said the In Between was dangerous. Was it possible to find food there?

More and more questions arose. Why did a portal to the In Between appear in our apartment at the bed-and-breakfast in Key West, as well as here? I had thought it was some freakish feature of my new inn, something related to hauntings and supernatural energies belonging to the place.

Was there some special connection between the In Between and me? Was it my fault that the portal had appeared in Key West and took away my husband? If so, why? What did it have to do with me?

I frantically called Missy, but she didn't answer. It was after sunset, so she was probably with a vampire patient. An hour later, I tried again, without success. Finally, she called me back and my story gushed from me like a waterfall.

"Oh, my," she said. "It sure sounds like it may have been a gateway."

She asked me if I had ever seen an extra door there before. I assured her I had not.

"Maybe, as you say, there's a connection to you somehow, though I can't imagine why."

"I need to find out if Cory is there," I said desperately.

"Don't, under any circumstance, enter a door to the attic if one shows up again. I mean it. You won't survive."

"Does that mean Cory didn't survive?"

"Darla, you need to accept the fact that if he did, in fact, go to the In Between, he may have died there. I don't mean to sound cruel, but there's a reason he hasn't returned in a year. Yes, there's the slight possibility he is trying to return, but, most likely, he passed away. Or he came back somewhere else on earth and didn't want to return to Key West."

That possibility was just a bad as him walking out on me.

"I'll try to make it up there again as soon as I can," Missy said. "Not that I can do much, but I'll be with you and help as much as I'm able to. In the meantime, don't obsess over this."

"Right. Good luck with that."

"And remember, don't go through a gateway. Your death won't help anyone."

"Okay. I promise."

"Keep your mind focused on other things. You have an inn to open. You need some income before you go broke. Concentrate on that. Keep busy. All right?"

"Yes, I will. Thank you, Missy."

She had a point. I had a tremendous amount of work to do here. I couldn't get diverted by desperate, unrealistic hopes. I had to stick with the task at hand.

Which was to turn a nearly 300-year-old building into an inn again. A building with mysterious portals to another plane of existence, a talking gargoyle, a vampire in a crawlspace, and who knows how many ghosts.

Something brushed against my calf. I looked down.

Let me make a correction: a nearly 300-year-old building with all of the above plus a stray black cat who wanted to stick around.

In short, a building that was now my home.

I decided then and there to change the name from the Hidalgo Inn, to the Esperanza Inn.

Because *esperanza* was Spanish for hope.

THE END

WHAT'S NEXT

GET A FREE E-BOOK

Sign up for my newsletter and get *Hangry as Hell*, a humorous paranormal novella, for free. Find out more about Darla's cousin, Missy, and her crazy life wrangling retired vampires, werewolves, and other monsters. You'll be the first to know about my new releases and lots of free book promotions. The newsletter is delivered only a couple of times a month. No spam at all, and you can unsubscribe at any time. Sign up to get your free book at wardparker.com.

ENJOYED THIS BOOK? PLEASE LEAVE A REVIEW

In the Amazon universe, the number of reviews readers leave can make or break a book. I would be very grateful if you could spend just a few minutes and write a fair and honest review. It can be as short or long as you wish. Thank you so much!

NEXT IN THE MEMORY GUILD MYSTERIES
The Psychic Touch

Psychic seeking psycho.

My name is Darla, and I'm a psychometrist.

When I touch objects, I pick up the memories and emotions of other people who have touched them.

I was recruited to serve on the Memory Guild, a secret society of supernaturals and paranormals. Based in one of the nation's oldest cities, the Guild preserves historical memory while fighting lies and conspiracy theories.

And now a psychopath is trying to assassinate the members of the Guild. Including yours truly.

With the reluctant help of a handsome detective, I try to find out who's behind the attacks. In between that, and trying to stay alive, I also have a day job: running a historic bed-and-breakfast. So I'm kind of busy right now.

I don't need unplanned trips though a magic portal and revealed secrets about my second husband who left me. All while dealing with my wacky witch mother and my trouble-prone daughter.

I'm your typical overworked woman. Except I also have a price on my head.

Get *The Psychic Touch* on Amazon or at wardparker.com

HAVE YOU READ FREAKY FLORIDA?
Check out this series of humorous paranormal mysteries featuring Darla's cousin, Missy.
Centuries-old vampires who play pickleball. Aging were-

wolves who surf naked beneath the full moon. Plus dragons, demons, ghouls, and more. They're all in Florida, land of the weird, where even monsters come to retire. That's how Missy Mindle comes in. She's started over in midlife as a home health nurse for elderly monsters and as a witch with growing powers. She uses her magick to solve mysteries, with a little help from a cute reporter. But dangerous secrets from the parents she never knew keep bubbling up.

You can start with a free novella when you sign up for my newsletter at wardparker.com

Or, dive right into Book 1, *Snowbirds of Prey*. Find it on Amazon or wardparker.com

ABOUT THE AUTHOR

Ward is a Florida native and author of the Freaky Florida series, a romp through the Sunshine State with witches, vampires, werewolves, dragons, and other bizarre, mythical creatures such as #FloridaMan. His newest series is the Memory Guild midlife paranormal mysteries. He also pens the Zeke Adams Series of Florida-noir mysteries and The Teratologist Series of historical supernatural thrillers. Connect with him on social media: Twitter (@wardparker), Facebook (wardparkerauthor), BookBub, Goodreads, or wardparker.com

ALSO BY WARD PARKER

The Zeke Adams Florida-noir mystery series. You can buy *Pariah* and *Fur* on Amazon or wardparker.com

The Teratologist series of historical paranormal thrillers. Buy the first novel on Amazon or wardparker.com

"Gods and Reptiles," a Lovecraftian short story. Buy it on Amazon or wardparker.com

"The Power Doctor," a historical witchcraft short story. Get it on Amazon or wardparker.com

Made in the USA
Monee, IL
01 June 2021

69967534R00146